passion over pride

KARMEN LEE

CONTENT NOTES

Here are a few notes for what you'll come across in this story. No spoilers intended, just so you know what you are getting into. Feel free to skip ahead if you don't want to read over these notes.

This read discusses the death of a parent, parental neglect, homophobia, biphobia, infidelity, on-the-page sex scenes, and breathplay.

Chapter One

Jonathan

I stared ahead, musing on the best way to hide a goddamn body. It wasn't something I often considered, but at this point, it was the only outcome I craved after two months of utter incompetence. Patience was not one of my virtues, so I didn't understand why everyone decided to test me. My stance on foolishness was well-established, yet day after day, bullshit seemed to pop up in each department. It was like karma was seeking retribution for some colossal infraction. I didn't believe in all that, but with how much of a bastard my father was, I wouldn't put it past the universe to cook some shit up just to get even.

"Who do you report to?"

The question was one I found myself asking more as of late as I attempted to fill in the gaps of my knowledge when it came to running Dummond Enterprises. How this company—the legacy that was truly the only thing my father probably ever loved—managed to run was anyone's guess. I had spent the past few months just putting out fires. The man in front of me—Kevin, I vaguely remembered him saying—blinked twice, looking strangely owl-like before responding. It was one blink too many, and I felt my patience growing thinner.

"I used to report to Curtis in accounting, but I was transfer—"

"On whose authorization?"

His wide-eyed gaze was starting to grate, and I was quickly coming to regret my insistence on meeting with all the teams face-to-face. I knew with my new role as CEO coming on the heels of my father's death that making an appearance and reassuring all my employees that the sudden loss would not negatively impact their working lives was important in ensuring low turnover. I couldn't have the company appearing weak in the face of our many competitors. Father had done well at making connections, but he had done ever better at making enemies. His funeral had proven that tenfold. Those bastards had barely hidden their glee behind half-hearted condolences, but no doubt they could smell blood in the water. It would only take one whiff of vulnerability for them to circle like vultures waiting to pick us off.

"Sir?"

Feeling the muscle in my eye trying to tick, I took a deep breath. "Who authorized your transfer?"

Kevin frowned deeper. "You did, sir, by way of Mr. Braselton."

Braselton. I clenched my jaw as that name popped up again. This was the fifth fucking transfer I'd heard of that I didn't recall seeing come across my desk thanks to a man I barely remembered the face for. I had slowly been weeding out the holdovers from father's reign who were collecting substantial paychecks for doing fuck all, and he clearly was one who needed to be snipped before he made me resort to homicide. I would have been surprised one man could cause so many problems if not for having seen the power some men wielded firsthand.

I gave Kevin a steady look. It wasn't his fault I was in a shit mood. It had been a long few months with a learning curve that shouldn't have been half as steep as it was. Damn father and his incessant need to hold everything close to his goddamn chest. Even knowing he was dying, he had kept his secrets regarding the business. Sure, he probably thought he would have more time to trickle out some truths before his ultimate demise, but clearly that hadn't panned out. Now, it was like he was trying to keep secrets from the grave. I had been training to step into this position for years, yet I still felt so ill-equipped to handle the change in weight on my shoulders.

It was almost enough to make me wish I could bring the bastard back just to kill him myself.

"Is this the position you want to be in? Project management?"

He looked like he wanted to say yes until I narrowed my eyes. I had no use for those here to get a paycheck by doing the bare fucking minimum. I didn't expect any of the employees to give more of a shit than me or my siblings did about the company we inherited, but I didn't want anyone around who couldn't at least be forthright about what their strengths and weaknesses were. I gave him a moment to think about his answer and looked over Kevin's previous performance reviews. On paper, he had done some good work. No write-ups. No performance improvement plans. He was the type of employee I wouldn't hesitate to reward. So, what the hell went wrong?

Braselton.

With a sigh, I forced my face to soften. It would do no good to have the man too scared to string a sentence together, and that wasn't the type of environment I had any desire to cultivate, regardless of what the rumors said. I was not my father. I had no need to be loved, but I had even less interest in being feared by my employees. Begrudging respect would work just fine as long as everyone did what they were hired to do and left me the fuck alone.

"Your performance until now has been excellent," I said, giving him something to work with so we could move this meeting along and I could put out the next fire on my hands. "Your previous supervisor, Curtis, expressed reservations about having you transferred from accounting and stated he had been eyeing you to replace him when he goes out for retirement next year."

That bit of information had Kevin sitting up straighter, and I made a note that positive praise was something he responded very well to. I suppose we had that in common. Some of the color came back into his cheeks, and with his shaggy hair, he looked a lot like a golden retriever. If he had a tail, it would probably be wagging.

"So, knowing that, please explain to me how you managed to miss the deadline for transferring the data to the review team?"

He ducked his head slightly, but as if he realized I was only looking for an explanation and not to cast blame, he lifted his head again. The determination in his eyes was a good sign. It gave me something I could work with.

"I was unaware the deadline existed," Kevin replied. "It wasn't until a couple days later that I was provided with the updated process documents that should have been given to me when I was transferred. The naming conventions were not the best, leading to confusion on the most updated files to pull from."

I nodded before looking back down at my notes. That was a plausible explanation, given what I had found when looking through the files myself. It was part of why the previous project manager had been let go in the first place. "I see. Well, it's good you recognized where the error was so it can be fixed before it creates bigger problems. For now, I am reversing your transfer and placing you back on Curtis's team. While it is a good thing you discovered a flaw in the team's protocols, I think your talents would be better served back in accounting, given our upcoming projects."

"Thank you, sir. I agree, sir." He stood when I did, and I extended my hand across my desk.

"Feel free to use tomorrow morning to move your things. I'll have Gregory expedite the transfer back, and all should be completed by tomorrow afternoon. Curtis will get you back up to speed on our upcoming deadlines." I shook his hand firmly as he apologized and thanked me again before herding him out of my office. Comforting silence was left in his wake, and I sighed in relief at having a few moments to myself. When I heard my office door open again, only the thought that it was an employee kept me from telling the person to get the fuck out.

"Was there something you forgot to mention?"

"About what?"

I glanced behind me and found my younger brother, Jameson, standing in the doorway. A little of my annoyance melted away when I realized it was just him and no one else. "Never mind. I thought you were Kevin."

"Who is Kevin?"

I waved his question away. "Unimportant. Was there something you needed?"

Jameson raised an eyebrow. "Do I need an excuse to come say hello to my big brother?"

My snort was loud, and my lips twitched when he chuckled. It wasn't unheard of for him to seek me out for one reason or another, but that didn't usually happen during work hours. I walked back around my desk and sat down. Jameson dropped into the chair across from me and fixed me with a look.

"I thought your office would be bigger."

"I was supposed to take over father's, but I decided to turn it into another conference room." The moment I had stepped into that office with the intention of moving into it, I had promptly walked out again. It felt wrong to use it for myself, not just because it was roughly three times larger than my current office that was already large enough to fit a desk, two chairs, and a full-size couch but also because it was *his*. I wasn't ready to step into that. "This office has suited me just fine for the past fifteen years, and I'm comfortable here."

"You always did have a thing about nesting," Jameson teased. Still, I knew he understood. Even after offering to have his entire office moved into the building, he had declined, instead choosing to merge his company into Dummond Enterprises in legality only. As much as he denied he was anything like our father, that stubborn streak was all dad.

It was impressive and fucking annoying when Jameson dug in his heels. Not much could move him at that point unless you had something better to dangle in front of him like an offering. Hell, half the time he still refused just for shits and giggles. It used to drive our parents to distraction when we were kids and even more so when we became adults. I had always found it amusing.

"Anyway, I wanted to talk to you about mom." He slouched down in the chair and folded his arms. "Have you talked to her?"

"Not for weeks," I replied honestly. Communication with her had been sporadic at best since father's funeral. Having time to mourn and grieve was important, so I didn't begrudge her need for space.

Jameson sighed.

"That's what everyone else said when I asked them. Even Jalissa hasn't talked to her in a week."

I frowned at that. It was unusual for mom to ignore Jalissa, who had always been her favorite. She might have ignored the rest of us, but she would have at least texted Jalissa. "Should we contact someone?"

"Already have." He hesitated before speaking again. "I know a guy."

That was enough to make me raise both eyebrows. "You know a guy?" I smirked. "Did you hire a private investigator to spy on our mother?"

"I didn't hire one," he denied. "He owed me a favor, so he's doing it for free."

"At least there isn't a paper trail." I leaned back in my chair and looked out the window. The sun was starting to set on the Atlanta skyline, painting the world in oranges and pale yellows. Soon enough, glittering lights would take over, but I planned to be out of here before that happened. "Do you think something is going on?"

Jameson shrugged. "No idea. You know how mother is. Secretive about the most random shit. We'll find out whatever it is eventually."

I nodded as I watched him settle back into his seat. The changes in Jameson were clear to see. He no longer seemed so tense. I knew father's death had been a relief to him in a way, and I didn't begrudge him that feeling. Things hadn't been easy growing up, especially for him. It was good to see him surer of himself instead of the over-the-top posturing he used to engage in.

"You look good."

He smirked at me before acknowledging my words. "Is there something you need?"

"No," I replied. "I just meant you seem…different. In a good way." I tacked the last words on to make sure he knew I was giving him a compliment and not insulting him.

"Love can do that to you, I guess."

Love. Yes, he is in love. I had known about Jameson's infatuation with his best friend's little sister, McKenzie. I had met her once or twice years before, but after she accompanied Jameson to the funeral, they had become damn near inseparable. Knowing Jameson, it was probably more on his end than hers. I loved my brother, but he could be clingier than goddamn molasses if you let him.

"Love," I said, rolling the word around on my tongue. It was mostly unfamiliar to me, but it did call to mind one memory. A memory of whispered words and thoughts of the future.

A future that had never come to pass.

"Yeah," he replied, leaning forward. "I know you don't do feelings and all that shit, but even you have heard of it. Or are the rumors true? Is Jonathan Jr. a dead-hearted bastard?"

I snorted. "I thought it was cold-hearted?"

"Nah, they swear your heart doesn't even exist. As much as I know it isn't true, I have to admit the gossip is amusing at times."

I shrugged. "If you say so." He was quiet as I shut my computer down and stood. "Was there anything else you needed?"

Jameson stood as well. "A drink, as do you. Come on, I'm buying."

~*~*~

Juliet's was busy as we stepped through the doors, but owning the management group for it had its perks and we were shown to a table right away. If I had been on my own, I would have sat at the bar for a drink or two before leaving, but Jameson vetoed that suggestion. Once we were seated with drinks in hand, I felt myself relaxing slightly. It had been a long week, and it was only fucking Wednesday. I didn't even want to think about what was in store for me tomorrow when I found myself face-to-face with that bastard Michael Braselton.

"What are you doing tomorrow?"

Jameson looked over his whisky glass with an arched brow. "Why?"

"I need you to keep me from killing someone."

That had him putting the glass down as the other eyebrow joined its twin. I knew my delivery of that line would get him, but I wasn't sure myself how much was truth and how much was jest.

"Yeah, okay. I had invited you out to ask your thoughts about something, but now I'm thinking you need—"

"No," I said, interrupting him. "You invited me, so you talk first. My thoughts will hold."

Jameson gave me a considering look before nodding sharply. "If you say so, brother. But I don't want to turn on the news tomorrow and see you being led away in cuffs." I didn't bother responding to that and waved off his words before taking a sip of my own drink as he spoke again.

The bourbon was smoky and smooth, and it set the mood. The dim lighting had me relaxing further, and Jameson's voice faded into the background. I threw out a comment when needed, but mostly, I let him talk. It was a familiar routine that had begun again in the weeks since we began fulfilling the charge of leading the company into whatever the future held. I felt a sense of peace at being able to share the bullshit with my siblings.

All of them.

There had been a moment after the reading of the will where I thought Jameson would contest, not to get more but to get less. It was no secret he'd struck out on his own to distance himself from the Dummond name, but I felt relieved that he had come back.

"Oh, shit."

"What?"

Jameson gestured behind me. I turned to look and nearly choked on my next sip when I saw just what had caught his attention.

No, not what.

Who.

Regina goddamn Mayfield was here.

Karma really was a bitch.

Chapter Two

Regina

Coming home again felt a lot like when I had left—unwanted but necessary. In the decade I'd been gone, lots of things had changed. I had, that was fucking sure.

And too many things stayed the same.

Walking into *Juliet's* had been a test of patience. I would have preferred to meet elsewhere, but this was where Christa had told me to go, and I wasn't about to argue so soon. I needed to get on her good side if I wanted this distribution deal to go through. She wasn't the one brokering it, but since it was with her father's company, I knew getting in good with her would come with perks. That meant playing the part of dutiful friend and kissing a little ass here and there until the ink on the contracts was dry.

Still, she could have chosen anywhere, yet she picked a place owned by the family who had forced my hand in this. Granted, they did own a lot of bars and restaurants in this city so logically, I knew I shouldn't fault her too much. Logic often got overruled by the need to be petty, but in this instance, I had to put a lid on it.

"Follow me, please."

I nodded to the waitress and folded my purse under my arm. As we passed the bar, a few men glanced my way, their eyes heavy as they looked me up and down. I smiled at a couple, not wanting to appear too standoffish, though I hoped they would keep their comments to themselves for the night. I didn't have it in me to play the polite princess this evening, but I wasn't trying to be a memorable presence just yet either.

We had just gotten beyond the bar when I felt another set of eyes on me. When I turned to look, I cursed the universe because what were the fucking odds?

"Fucking hell," I hissed under my breath as my eyes met a familiar gaze. Jonathan Dummond Jr. Of all the goddamn days to run into him, it had to be this one. After taking a deep breath, I pasted on a sharp smile. My sister, Casey, always said this particular smile made me look like a bitch. It was one of my favorites.

"Well, this is a surprise," I said evenly as we came up to Jonathan's table. I glanced at Jameson. "Jameson, it's good to see you again."

He stood up with a smile, and we exchanged a quick hug. His smile was wide and friendlier than it had any right to be, given my history with his family. Then again, it wasn't his fault, and I knew he'd had his own problems with the senior Dummond.

"You look amazing," he said, giving me a quick look up and down. There was nothing but friendliness in his gaze, which I appreciated. I knew I looked good, but what woman wasn't happy to hear that? Jameson was a good-looking guy with wide shoulders, smooth dark skin, and a boyish smile. Still, I had to begrudgingly admit that the man beside him held my attention even more.

"Hello, Jonathan."

"Regina." Jonathan's voice was like the darkest chocolate. It was the kind of voice romance novels were made to be read by, and it was so fucking unfair it made me want to key something. He didn't reach out for a hug, and I didn't offer. "You look...well."

Jameson's snort kept me from saying what I wanted to say, and instead, I smiled. "As do you. My condolences on the loss of your father."

"Thank you." He didn't say anything else, and I didn't offer anything more. They would have been empty platitudes for a man I was glad was dead.

"It was good to see you both," I said finally before moving on. I could still feel that gaze on my back, and I fought off a shiver. It wouldn't do to seem affected by someone who had the emotional range of a wet bag of cement. Jonathan might have been attractive, but that and money were the only things he had going for him.

The only thing I wanted was revenge, but I knew I would have to play my cards right. There was too much riding on this to fuck up by being too impulsive. There were levels to this game, and I planned on playing to win.

"Oh my gosh, Regina!" Christa's enthusiasm was grating, but I pushed away my annoyance and responded in kind, accepting her hug with one of my own. Her blue eyes twinkled as she stepped back and gestured to the man beside her. "This is my fiancé, Marcello, and his friend, Liam."

I shook both men's hands and eyed Liam for a moment. I knew exactly who he was, of course, but I hadn't expected him to be as attractive as he was. When his gaze went hooded, I let my smile reply in kind.

"It's a pleasure to meet you." His voice was pleasant, though it did nothing for me. Still, it was better this way. I needed to stay focused, and I couldn't do that if I wanted to fall into bed with him.

"The pleasure is all mine," I replied. Once we were seated, I kept up the charade of being interested. I had pretended not to know that Christa was setting this up as a double date of sorts. Truthfully, meeting like this was often more useful than meeting in a business capacity. People were more likely to let things slip when they were relaxed and among friends.

Despite the conversation going on around me, I could still feel those eyes. I used my glass to cover my motions as I glanced to the side. Annoyance burned through me when I saw Jonathan's gaze trained on me. What the hell was he playing at?

"It seems you have another admirer."

I turned my head slowly and tried to bury my thoughts. Christa was smiling like she knew something I didn't, which couldn't have been further from the truth. Marcello nodded, and I feigned a bored expression as I turned to look at Jonathan. With a smile, I lifted my glass in acknowledgment. Ignoring him would have drawn more attention to things, and that wasn't what I wanted. Liam was my target tonight, and I needed my plan to go off without a hitch. If Jonathan fucked that up for me, I would shove my glass down his throat.

Jonathan raised his glass, mirroring me, and when Jameson turned, he smiled and did the same.

"I doubt that," I said finally before turning away. "I heard Jameson is practically married at this point, and Jonathan's lack of interest in anyone is well-known."

Christa nodded. "True. I was so surprised when I heard Jameson was dating some author. She's probably just after his money or something." She shook her head as if the very thought of him dating someone he actually liked was absurd. Then again, I knew for a fact that her and Marcello had been a match arranged by both of their families. Really, I didn't think she had a fucking leg to stand on, but I kept my thoughts on that to myself. "I can't even imagine what they must have to talk about."

I chuckled along with them to keep up appearances even though I wanted to smother them all. Liam leaned toward me, and I forced myself to continue playing the part of someone who was interested.

"That dress suits you perfectly." It was a comment I had heard plenty of times. "I bet you would look just as perfect out of it."

I giggled softly, but inside, I wanted to wrap my hands around his throat and squeeze. "I don't think that's what good boys say on a first date." From the corner of my eye, I could see Christa smiling. She no doubt thought she had facilitated the perfect match. She was right in a way. Pairing me with Liam was exactly what I wanted.

"Who says I'm a good boy?"

Got you, I thought to myself. Men are easy. Show a little leg and giggle and most of them will fall into your hand with ease. Still, there was one man who seemed to defy that. It was part of the reason I planned on staying as far away from him as possible until I had all my pieces in place.

Jonathan Dummond was my end goal, and I was going to win, no matter what.

~*~*~

The sun had no business being as bright as it was, and I frowned as I pulled my glasses over my eyes. The night had been successful enough, though there was a moment I worried it was all crashing down when I declined to go home with Liam. He'd been hinting at getting me into his bed and between his sheets for most of the evening. I didn't have anything against sleeping with him to get what I wanted, but not yet. I was exhausted and hadn't had it in me to lie back and make it believable. Guys like him only knew how to fuck one way—selfishly, with a lot of grunting and not enough pushing. I had enough disappointment in life, and I wasn't trying to add more so soon.

The streets of Suwanee were surprisingly clear for a Saturday. I had expected there to be a lot more going on, but I was also appreciative of it. I hadn't been back since leaving years ago, but even I remembered how terribly people drove. It made me long for walkable streets and public transportation that worked. Living in London hadn't been perfect, but at least I hadn't needed to risk my life or my sanity behind the wheel unless I really wanted to.

Getting to Casey's house took longer than I wanted, and by the time I let myself in, I was hungry enough to damn near keel over. "I hope breakfast is ready, otherwise someone might get hurt."

"Auntie Gigi!"

A loud shout was my only warning before I almost found myself on my ass. Twin sets of arms wrapped around my knees, and I looked down, smiling. "You two need to give Gigi a little warning before you try to take me out."

"Hi, auntie." Sticky hands reached up, and I gripped them before they made contact with my white blouse. "We made you pancakes."

"Thank you, Malachi," I replied, pitching my voice higher. His twin, Malik, stayed quiet, but his dark brown eyes stared up at me. He smiled, and I chuckled at the space between his teeth where the two front ones should be. "I know you and Malik did a great job. I can't wait to eat them."

Before I could say anything more, Casey stuck her head around the corner. "If y'all don't let her go and come sit, no one is getting pancakes."

That threat did it, and as quickly as they came, they went, feet slapping against the hardwood floors as they disappeared from sight. I snorted and followed, pushing my sunglasses up onto my head and dropping my purse and keys on the foyer table. The air was thick with the smell of crackling bacon and home. A deep longing burned in my chest as the familiar scent reminded me of days long past, but I pushed the thoughts away and walked into the kitchen.

Sunlight poured in from the floor-to-ceiling Georgia windows. Casey was at the stove, and I smiled when the sound of popping oil was followed by a heated curse. "If mama was here, she'd threaten you with a bar of soap and a switch."

She glared at me over her shoulder. "Well, it's a good thing she isn't here then, bitch. And don't you go telling her anything either, otherwise I'll let her know exactly how you spent your first night back in town."

I held my hands up in surrender, but the smile that split my lips was genuine. I had missed this easy camaraderie while I was dealing with my unwanted exile. Casey had stayed in Georgia though she had laid low, quietly marrying and transitioning into the life of a stay-at-home mom. It had been a battle convincing her to come back to Atlanta, and she had been adamant about taking no part in whatever I was scheming. I had let it be. She had a family and kids to worry about now. I didn't need her getting messed up in my business. Plausible deniability was the name of the game.

"Where's Ray?" I held out my hand for the platter of bacon she was plating. "I didn't see his car out front."

"He had to head to the office for some emergency meeting," she replied before following me to the dining table where Malachi and Malik were practically vibrating in their seats. Eggs, toast, and grits were already on the table, steam rising attractively and making my mouth water. The food in London was good, but I still missed the down South cooking that could only be found in cast iron with a container of Crisco and the whispers of your ancestors. "Some mess is apparently going down with one of their clients, and of course, they called him in."

I shook my head but didn't say anything else. What Ray did was his own business. I didn't dislike him. He and his family had taken Casey in without a thought, and for that, I would always be grateful. But I couldn't deny I was also slightly resentful she hadn't come with me to Europe. Then again, she wasn't the one who had been foolish enough to get involved with the Dummonds in the first place and fuck things up for everyone.

"More food for us, right, my little crotch goblins?"

"Please don't call them that."

Malik giggled and whispered to Malachi. I could see what was coming, and I had a moment to cover my mouth with my hand before I lost my shit.

"Crotch goblin!"

Malachi's screech did me in, and I had to put my head down to smother my cackles of glee. Kids were fucking hilarious, and I loved riling my nephews up. I looked up when Casey sat opposite me. Her look told me exactly how she felt about that little outburst, and I shushed Malachi quickly before she decided feeding me wasn't in the cards.

Once we had eaten and the boys bounced off to their playroom, quiet settled around me, and I thought about the past few days. I was still hesitant about what I did and didn't tell Casey, but I couldn't help but need a sounding board, and she had always been my go-to.

"Do you think I should have stayed away?"

Beside me, Casey paused, her hands covered in suds as she carefully washed each dish. She moved again, handing me the plate before grabbing another from the soapy water. I rinsed it before setting it on the drying rack without comment.

I knew she would need a moment to formulate her response, and I appreciated the time she took to think it out. I couldn't afford to be rash about this.

"No," she said finally. She turned to look at me, and the same determination I saw in my own gaze each morning was reflected in hers. She might not have dealt with all the same consequences as me, but I knew things hadn't been easy for her. "It was time for you to come back."

I nodded. No other words were needed, and none were said. Coming back to Atlanta had been on my mind since the moment I left. I had played my cards carefully and kept my complaints to myself. I had dealt with the sharp comments from our parents and especially the extended family. Luckily enough, our mother's side of the family in London had been more than welcoming. Our uncle, Edward, had been especially lovely as he helped me learn the business of planning for the future. It was his advice that had given me the push I needed to secure my spot as Vice President of Mayfield Group and make my way back here.

"Regardless, I'm glad you're back," Casey continued, pulling my attention. "I missed you. I know you had to leave, and I chose to stay, but not having you around has been hard."

"I know," I replied, leaning my shoulder against hers. "I missed you too. Seeing you once a year wasn't enough." It hadn't been, but I had made do. Our parents had been forced to upgrade the internet just to accommodate the hours-long Skype calls Casey and I had. It wasn't unusual for us to be on and connected from sunup to sundown regardless of if we were in front of the computer or not.

Casey and I weren't twins. In fact, we were two years apart. But she was my best friend, and moving without her had been almost maddening. "But I'm back, and I don't plan on going anywhere."

She smiled. "Really? There were no sexy European men grandma tried to set you up with? I find that hard to believe."

She wasn't wrong. Our maternal grandmother was not a shy woman when it came to what she wanted or what she wanted for you. I'd had to learn how to outsmart her quickly without offending her. It had taken a few years to perfect, but by the time she caught on, I was already making plans to return to Atlanta.

"Oh, you know she did. She's still mad you married some random American like mom. She was hoping I'd at least find a footballer to settle down with in France or Spain."

Casey chuckled and shook her head. "That woman and her football."

We settled into quiet again as we finished cleaning the morning's dishes. When Casey leaned her head on my shoulder, I returned the gesture, leaning my head on hers. "Just be careful."

I didn't want to promise her anything I couldn't keep. I knew the dangers in playing this game with people who had more money than shame. But if we were going to get back the money and prominence that was stolen from us, it was a game I had to play to the fullest.

"I'll do my best."

Chapter Three

Jonathan

Meetings were the fucking worst. I understood the point of them, and I even set up some of them myself. But when I only had twenty-four hours in a day and half of that was taken up by people who talked for the sake of talking, it was enough to make me wish all this shit was a fucking email.

Now was an example of just how distasteful I found them. I had hoped having a discussion over lunch would result in concise commentary and more focus on the food in front of us, but every bite seemed to bring more words flooding from Michael Braselton's mouth. The man was even more irritating in person than he was in hearing about him in passing. With a mental sigh, I focused back in on the one-sided conversation.

"I told him that to increase profits, we needed to cut some of the dead weight from the other departments and gave him a list of names to choose from." His words caught my attention, and I froze with my fork in the air.

"I wasn't aware there was an issue with our profits." Cycling back through the conversations I'd had with our accounting department brought nothing glaring to the surface. "A dip in growth is to be expected when leadership changes. It shouldn't require anything as major as eliminating personnel unless there's something I'm missing."

"Oh, of course," he replied with a smile that looked as fake as the Rolex on his wrist. "I would never imply you were out of the loop on anything. I'm just looking out for our shareholders. They expect positive growth, and if that means trimming down the number of people we have on payroll—"

"Who authorized you to make decisions regarding personnel?" I let my voice go sharp in the way that reminded me of my father. It was a tone I had come to hate during my childhood, but I couldn't deny it got the job done. Michael paused and blinked quickly, betraying just how much I caught him off guard. I was aware of the role he'd played while my father was in charge, and I had zero desire for any of that to continue under my watch. Trust was a big deal to me, and I didn't trust him to tell me I was being pissed on.

He seemed to regain his footing rather quickly, and it was then I knew this bitch had to go. Michael took a sip of his drink before speaking again. "Well, as you know, your late father authorized me to help with the—"

"He authorized you to single-handedly make personnel decisions without needing to relay that information to him? I find that hard to believe." I knew my words and suspicions were true when he looked around as if scrambling for how best to answer.

"Well, not exactly. I provided him with reports to explain my rationale and the results after—"

"Wonderful," I said, cutting him off. "I'd like the documentation from the past six months of which personnel was let go or reassigned, the reasons behind it, and evidence to support your decision-making process."

"Jonathan, I hardly see the reason behind—"

"A week should be enough time to pull that information together since you normally compile it as is. Correct?" That had his mouth snapping shut, but I didn't let my expression betray my thoughts. I knew I was painting him into a corner, and I was sure he was aware of it as well. When Michael nodded, I continued. "Wonderful. I look forward to reading your report."

My tone left no room for argument, and without hesitation I continued eating, hoping this would mark the end of his chattiness. Awkward meals were nothing to me, having grown up dealing with my share of them. I hardly remembered a family meal not being plagued by at least residual awkwardness once I was old enough to read the room. After I finished my food, I signaled to the waitress for the check, waving off Michael's half-hearted attempts to pay.

He quickly dismissed himself, and once he disappeared out the door, it was like a weight came off my shoulders. I had been brought up knowing the company my father built would fall into my hands one day, but I hadn't expected it to come so soon or with so much bullshit to deal with.

I thanked the waitress and left her a large enough tip to hopefully make up for bearing witness to such a tension-filled conversation. The day was still young, and I needed to get back to the office to handle a few more phone calls. I was on my way out the door when a figure caught my eye. I fought my desire to scowl as karma once again decided to stomp on my patience.

"Regina." I didn't remember telling myself to walk over to the bar, and yet here I was. She turned, and the fire in her gaze almost had me reaching out to feel that warmth. "It's good to see you again."

Her lips curled up in a twisted version of a smile. "Interesting you would say that." She turned more fully. "What are you doing here?"

I raised an eyebrow. "Well, I'm pretty sure I own the restaurant." It was one of many in my portfolio, and dining at it meant I could enjoy a meal and check up on things in one swoop.

"There you are." A new voice entered, and I turned in time to see Liam Bolden step forward. He glanced at me, and I felt my hackles rise. What the fuck was he doing here? "Jonathan, good to see you, my man. How's business going?"

"The same as always," I replied easily. The Boldens weren't unknown to me, but it was unusual to run into Liam outside of garden parties or golf courses down in Savannah. His father and mine had been in business together at one point, but that dissolved in a fiery blaze of hurt feelings and accusations. Things had apparently been resolved by the time my father died, but I didn't plan to rebuild that bridge of business anytime soon. Rumors of the Boldens' underhanded dealings had picked up lately and didn't jive with the changes I planned on implementing before the year was through.

But that still left the question of why Regina and Liam were dining together in one of my restaurants.

"I'm surprised you two know each other," I said before nodding to the bartender. Work could wait while I got to the bottom of this. Regina glared at me but didn't say anything when the bartender slid over my glass. "Atlanta seems to be a small world these days."

Liam glanced at Regina before turning his snake-like smile to me. When the bartender slid another glass to him, he nodded. "It does seem that way, doesn't it? What brings you in today?"

"Just handling some internal business. You know how that goes."

"I do," he agreed before taking a sip. Over the rim of his glass, his eyes never left mine, and I followed suit. I normally didn't allow myself to get into pissing contests, but something about the way his gaze slid over Regina had me wanting to tell him to meet me outside. It was caveman shit, but damn would it feel good to break his face and let out a little frustration. "I'm sort of here on business myself."

"Oh?" Regina said, her tone stopping me short. "Is that what I am now?" The flirty smile on her face had me clenching my jaw. It wasn't that I wasn't familiar with it, I just wasn't used to it being turned toward anyone but me. By the look on her face, I could tell she knew just what I was thinking.

Liam moved past me and set a folder on the bar. There was nothing to discern from the front of it, and though I wanted to ignore it, I was curious. Seeing Regina with Liam was jarring enough, but I didn't know if I preferred them to be together socially or business-wise. Neither meant anything good, a fact I knew I needed to explain to her.

"Regina, could I have a word with you for a moment?"

The look she gave me would have ripped off the balls of anyone else. I knew the fury it held, but it made me even more determined. After a moment, she nodded sharply.

"Excuse us for a moment, Liam. This won't take long." She smiled at him before standing up from her stool. I nodded at Liam before gesturing for Regina to follow me. I let my hand hover over the small of her back, heat bleeding through even with the few inches of space between us. As much as I wanted to let my hand connect, I knew my message wouldn't get through if I crowded her.

I led her down a dimly lit hallway and toward the manager's office. It was thankfully empty, and I shut the door behind us before locking it for good measure.

"What the fuck is your problem?"

I expected the vitriol. Deserved it, even. A decade of hurt feelings between us ensured that. "My problem is you being involved with someone as slimy as Liam Bolden. In what world does that make sense?"

Regina narrowed her eyes. "In the world where I'm trying to make up for the loss of more than half my family's assets. You have a lot of nerve talking about slimy businessmen, considering your father's reputation."

I didn't disagree, and I let her know that. "I am not my father."

"You are exactly like your father," she spit out, taking a step toward me. The air was thick, and I felt something in me twist. The accusation cut true and sliced at a part of me I had been trying to keep at bay. "You think just because you have money that you can do whatever the fuck you want, and we should all just fall in line. I refuse."

I stood frozen as she stepped closer. My muscles were tense and poised to snap, though I still wasn't sure what I planned to do until I felt her finger poke my chest. It was like all the frustration of the past few months exploded, and it wasn't until I had her wrist in my hand and my other arm around her waist that I realized I had moved.

With her pressed against me, I could feel the frantic rise and fall of our chests as we both took in heaving breaths. Pressure nearly choked me as her free hand wrapped around my throat, locking us in an embrace I wasn't sure I wanted to get out of. This close, I could see the fire in her eyes and count the lashes that framed them. This Regina wasn't the same shy girl who had disappeared from my life ten years ago. This Regina was a fighter, and the more she struggled, the more I realized I wanted to scorch myself on that flame.

"What are you doing with Liam?" I grit out, trying to bring my thoughts back to why I had pulled her in here to begin with. "Dirty business isn't who you are."

Her eyes narrowed.

"You don't know who the fuck I am, Jonathan." Before I could counter, lips soft and sure pressed against mine. I didn't bother thinking, my body reacting before my brain could catch up, and I pressed back.

This heat had haunted my dreams and stalked my nightmares. It was the presence I gorged myself on at night when I lay alone thinking about the what-ifs. My dick knew it well and pulsed at the thought of having it real and present in my arms after years of only fantasies. They were nothing compared to the reality of having Regina warm and solid in my arms.

"Get rid of him," I bit out, swallowing hard against the hand still at my neck.

A sharp squeeze had me groaning deep in the back of my throat before I bit a kiss against her mouth. I let go of her wrist in favor of gripping the back of her neck and angling her head to plunder between her lips. The taste of her was everything, and the hunger in me now was for more than food could fill. I needed her naked and under me. I needed her bare and over me.

A hand wiggled between our bodies, and my groan turned into a grunt of pain. "Don't tell me what the fuck to do." I opened my eyes. Regina's free hand was cupped around my dick, but the pressure was quickly skirting more into pain. "You think you have the leverage here when I literally have your dick in my hand? Your ego is clearly too damn big for your own good."

"You used to like that," I reminded her.

"I was young and naïve then. I thought you were someone you weren't. Now I know better."

I narrowed my eyes as I stared at her. I would be lying if I said I didn't deserve it. We had both been young and insecure and far too wrapped up in making sure we lived up to our own families' fucked-up legacies. But I wasn't the only one at fault here for the way our relationship had imploded. I wasn't the one who left without so much as a goodbye. I had thought I understood what might be going on, but it was clear I was missing something vital.

"What aren't you telling me?" The question was out before I could even pause to think. Jameson wasn't the only stubborn bastard in the family. I wouldn't rest until I figured out what was going on. "What happened to you?"

A knock on the door had us both shifting slightly, me with a wince at the strain her grip was putting on my balls. Regina glanced at the door behind us before focusing back on me. Her grip loosened slightly but didn't let go completely. Her lipstick was smeared, and I felt a bolt of pleasure at knowing that was because of me. I wasn't ashamed to walk out with the evidence of her all over me. My hold on the back of her neck tightened at the thought of anyone seeing the both of us in this state and putting together exactly what had happened.

"Are you in trouble?"

She glared at me for a moment longer before rolling her eyes and releasing me from her grip. The grip leaving my balls was a relief, but I wouldn't have minded the hand at my neck staying. I wisely kept that thought to myself and reluctantly loosened my own hold, letting her slide away from me. Cool air rushed in between us, and I hated it. That fire between us was one I had missed. One I had craved. The person on the other side of the door knocked again, and I called out.

"Oh, Mr. Dummond." I was slightly relieved to hear it was only the manager, Franklin. "I wasn't aware you were in. I can come back later."

I looked at Regina for a moment longer. Her expression gave nothing away, which left me unsettled and wanting a way to close this gap between us. I knew something must have happened, and I was sure it probably had something to do with my bastard of a father. Yet another reason for me to wish I could bring the man back just to put him six feet under again. All the shit happening kept coming right back to him. Convenient that he up and fucked off right when I needed to know what strings he had been pulling.

"It's fine, Franklin," I called out again. "We're just leaving." I opened the door, and sound spilled back into the room. The smile on Franklin's face dipped slightly when he saw Regina and I standing there. Before he could say anything, I turned to Regina.

"The ladies' lounge is the first door to your left." I pointed down the hallway opposite the direction of the dining area. "It was good to see you, Regina. I would love to catch up with you again, maybe over dinner?"

Her lips twitched before she glanced at Franklin. I thought for sure she was going to tell me to go to hell, but she just smiled slowly before giving a noncommittal hum. When she left, I could only watch her walk away. Franklin's presence kept me from doing anything other than watching and wondering just when the next shoe was going to drop.

Chapter Four

Regina

I stared into the mirror hoping for a sign of just what the fuck had happened. My lipstick was smeared up past my lip, and when I pressed my fingers to it, the heat was unimaginable. I could still feel the strength of Jonathan's arm around my waist as he held me close and the phantom length of his dick in my palm. Squeezing it hadn't been my first thought even as I had my other hand around his throat. I had imagined that would get him, and yet I still remembered the soft rumble that accompanied the action. The hand on the back of my neck had almost yanked a similar sound out of me.

This was going to be a problem. I hadn't been abstinent from sex, but I had been discreet about it. Long-term relationships had been off the table. I knew my parents had hoped I would find a nice, well-connected English man and settle down, but that wasn't in the cards. It wouldn't have been fair to have someone get attached to me when I didn't plan on staying long-term. Not now anyway. There was still too much unfinished business to take care of here, starting with Liam. That reminder had me back in motion.

I set my purse on the counter so I could pull out my makeup pouch. Five minutes later, my lips looked as luscious as before. The kisses Jonathan and I had shared had plumped them more, and I knew exactly what someone might be thinking when they looked at them. It was what I was going for—the right amount of sexual appeal to leave someone guessing and wondering just how it would feel to touch.

"Liam, I am so sorry about that," I said, pitching my voice softly as I walked back to the bar. Blessedly, Jonathan was nowhere to be found. I didn't need him sticking his nose into business that didn't have anything to do with him. I was a big girl. I could handle this shit myself, especially since it meant eventually circling back to him.

Liam looked me over for a moment before he smiled. "No problem at all. I understand how things go when the Dummonds are involved. They can be quite…overbearing, even on good days. Shall we head to our table?" He signaled to the bartender when I agreed, and soon enough, we were being led to one of the back tables that provided a lot more privacy from listening ears.

"So, I was surprised when you called me yesterday about wanting to get in on this," Liam began once our orders had been taken. "I thought the Mayfields were solely focused on the import and export of food goods."

I took a sip of my water to give myself a moment to remember my story. I wasn't falsifying much. Uncle Edward had always drilled in to keep the lie as close to the truth as possible, so it was easy to remember and expand upon. Keeping all the moving parts of this together was going to be tough enough without creating some elaborate story.

"We are, of course. But we are also eager to restart our restaurant group here in Atlanta with a focus on fine dining and the luxury experience," I replied. "Food is one of the biggest luxuries there can be, and I think now is the right time to capitalize on some amazing partners we have and see how we can shake up the Atlanta food scene. We just need the right…partnerships so we can secure locations and permits."

I looked up at him from under my lashes. It was tough to gauge his interest. He had happily met me today, but I wasn't yet sure if he realized I was serious about the business side or if he just thought he was going to be able to get in my panties. Then again, with just how quickly my body responded to Jonathan, fucking Liam might not be such a bad idea. At least it would remind me why sex with the men who ran in these circles was a bad move. Mixing business with pleasure never worked well. I had already learned that lesson once.

The conversation paused when the appetizer was brought, and the soft sounds of others talking and eating filtered in. When Liam spoke again, his voice was pitched low.

"I do believe a partnership with you would be worth my while in many ways." His gaze was heated, though it did nothing for me. There was no passion there. Only rugged determination to make this work, but it was better that way. I didn't need to forget my motivations. I looked down when he slid the folder over to me. I had noticed it earlier but wisely stayed quiet until he brought it up so as not to appear too eager.

I delicately put my hand down on the folder and thankfully didn't flinch when his covered mine. His fingers crept over the back of my hand and instead of pulling away like I wanted, I smiled.

"Is there something else you want to say?" I asked coyly. This whole thing was ruining my appetite, and I just wanted to take the folder and run. Liam's fingers slid up my wrist, and I shivered slightly. The way his eyes narrowed, I could tell he thought his touch was doing something for me, but really, that was a shiver of aversion. I was not a fan of being touched, especially by people I didn't like.

"Come over tonight," he said before licking his lips. "Once you read over those, call me, and I'll come pick you up. We'll have a lot to discuss."

I raised an eyebrow. "And this discussion can only occur at your home? Or is there something else you're after?" I slid my hand out from under his and pulled the folder toward me. When I went to open it, his hand came down gently.

"Don't open them yet." He leaned back in his chair as the waiter came with our entrées. "Let's eat and get to know one another, and then later, we can talk business."

I nodded and set the folder aside. "That sounds like a perfect proposition."

~*~*~

I sighed as I lowered myself into the water. Fragrant heat enveloped me, and I groaned as warmth seeped into my skin. The afternoon had been long and arduous between fending off Liam's increasingly insistent attempts at getting me into bed with him and making sense of the documents he'd provided me. Then there was the fact that every time I turned a corner, I felt myself tensing at the thought of running into Jonathan again. The memory of our kisses persisted even as I tried my best to push the thoughts away.

When I planned my return, I hadn't thought he would be this much of a problem so soon. I had expected to run into him at some point, given his family's prominence in the city's business scene, but seeing him this often was making me rethink things. Disappearing into random offices with him was not keeping a low profile, and I didn't want the wrong tongues to start wagging and fuck up my plans. I needed to get ahead of this before it got even more out of control. I lifted my hands, letting the water glide between my fingers.

The bath bomb I used left a lavender hue that grew lighter, then darker as I swirled the water around. My thoughts did the same as I mapped out a plan of attack. Maybe waiting to run into Jonathan was the wrong move. It wasn't like me to just wait around as is. Clearly, if I wanted to stay in control of this thing, I needed to switch gears and confront him head-on. That might even give me an edge in the long run.

When I got out of the bath half an hour later, I still didn't have any concrete plans for how to handle him showing up at inopportune times. One thing I was sure of was I would not be disappearing into any other offices or private rooms with him. As good as that kiss was—and fuck, was it good—I needed to stay away from him before I ended up wrapping more than just a hand around his neck. I couldn't deny I enjoyed when a man knew how to get on his knees and surrender.

My cell ringing shook me from my musings, and I wrapped a towel around me before walking back into my bedroom.

"Casey? Is everything alright?" I shifted when my towel started to slip and gripped it tighter. "This is kind of a late call for you."

"I think Ray is cheating on me."

Everything screeched to a halt, and I could swear even the blood in my veins paused at her words. I had to pull the phone away from my ear to look at it and make sure it was really Casey calling and not someone trying to troll me. Cheating? Ray? That didn't make any sense. Last I knew, the man practically worshipped the ground Casey walked on.

Watching them together had been sickening at first, but it had quickly been replaced by happiness that she had found something good in the mess that was our lives. If I were the jealous type, their relationship definitely would've done it for me.

"What are you talking about, Casey? How do you know Ray is cheating on you?" I tried to think fast, going over all my encounters with them, together and separate, to see if there was something I potentially missed. "Does he not know I'm your sister and that I would murder him for hurting you?"

In fact, I was pretty sure I said that to him once over FaceTime. I never hid how protective I was over my sister. Anyone who came into our lives just had to realize that.

"Can you come over?"

"Of course, I can. I'll be there as soon as I throw some clothes on." She thanked me quietly before hanging up, and as soon as the phone screen dimmed, I fell onto my couch in shock. This was not one of the squares on my annual bingo card of shit to do. I gave myself a moment to prepare mentally before I threw on some clothes and made my way down the interstate.

It took longer than I would've liked, but after a few curses and a quick thought that I should probably purchase a Peach Pass if I planned on making this a regular thing, I finally made it. I let myself in, not bothering to ring the bell to announce my presence. The house was eerily quiet, and I glanced around before making my way to the living room. I found Casey alone on the couch, head buried in her hands. The familiar burn of rage was welcome, and I let it carry me over to her.

"Casey," I called out, not wanting to startle her. She looked up, eyes red and wet with tears.

"I didn't know who else to call," she croaked out. I sat beside her and opened my arms. When she was this upset, I knew it was better to give her the option of comfort rather than just pushing it on her. I sighed in relief when she fell into my arms, her own wrapping tightly around my waist as she buried her face in my shoulder. I took a moment to gather myself and figure out what to say.

Infidelity had never been a part of our lives. Our parents had their own issues like anyone else, but to my knowledge, cheating never seemed to be one of them. Even after twenty-something years of marriage, the two of them still seemed disgustingly taken with one another despite the bullshit of the past decade. They were a unit, which had always been equal parts impressive and annoying when they both said no to things without hesitation. It was the same type of relationship I had thought Casey and Raymond enjoyed.

"So, explain to me why you think Ray is cheating," I said after a few moments of letting her get herself together. I grabbed the box of Kleenex that was already on the table and pulled out a couple sheets to hand to her. She mopped up her face as best she could before settling back against the cushion of the couch. I leaned back, pressing my shoulder against hers like I always did when showing my support.

"Well, you know how he's been working late, right?" she began. I nodded. "This isn't the first time he's had to stay late or meet someone late. But he always tells me where he's going to be, so I know whether to wait up for him. It's always about business, and he always says he feels bad about missing time away from the kids."

I nodded. That was something I had thought Ray and our dad had in common. There were plenty of times when Casey and I were younger that I remembered waiting up for our dad or being woken up at night when he got home just to spend some time with us.

"Tonight, he told me he was going to be meeting someone in Buckhead, and I didn't think anything of it until…" She trailed off.

I pushed her lightly to get her talking again. "Until what?"

Casey sighed before looking over at me. "Until one of the women from our friend group sent me this text." She held her phone out to me, and after a moment of hesitation, I took it.

Everything was there, live and in technicolor. I cycled through the messages, noting the pictures that, though grainy, did look like they were Ray. He was sitting in a restaurant I recognized. The next few photos were angled, and I saw that he was sitting with a woman. It could have been a business meeting except for how lowcut her top was. It was cute, but nothing about it screamed business. No. That was the type of top I wore when I had business of another sort on my mind. The woman and Ray looked a lot more comfortable than they had any right to be when he had a wife at home falling apart on their couch and two kids sleeping soundly without a thought to how their lives were potentially about to change.

"Are you sure that this person who sent you the pictures is trustworthy and not just trying to cause trouble?" I looked back up at her. "Don't get me wrong, the shit is sketchy as all hell, but maybe it really is a business meeting."

Casey shrugged, not looking the least bit placated. "She's not the type to just start shit, I don't think, but I also don't know her very well. Ray just got this promotion, and a lot of the friends we have now are new."

"So, you don't know much about them or how they operate?"

She nodded in agreement. "She seems nice enough, and the fact that she sent this to me rather than keeping it quiet says something, doesn't it?" She looked to me for confirmation. "I'm trying not to be naïve here, but I know how some of these groups move. They might cover things up for the sake of peace, but she told me immediately."

I hummed, not wanting to give voice to thoughts just yet that hadn't quite formed. I liked Ray and wanted to give him the benefit of the doubt, but I also didn't know their friends. I had heard of some of them, given that I was reestablishing myself in the Atlanta business world, but even so, some of them came from old money families, and that was not a group that was easy to penetrate. There was a stark difference in how old money treated new money, and right now, I wasn't in the realm of either.

From what I had heard from Casey, all the couples seemed nice enough. Very vanilla. Very suburban. Totally not my kind of people, but then again, it was the suburbs where secrets were often kept. You never really knew someone until you saw them at their worst. That was when the claws came out and people's true intentions became clear. Before then, it was all lip service.

"How long ago did she send you these pictures?" I asked.

"I don't know. Maybe an hour or so," Casey replied. "Why?"

I squinted again at the phone image. "Because I'm pretty sure I recognize this restaurant." I stood up, knowing there was at least one thing I could do. "If Ray is cheating, I want to catch that bastard in the act."

Casey stood with me as she reached for the phone. She clutched it in her hand and looked down at it. "What makes you think they'll even still be there? They might have already left to some hotel somewhere." Her hands shook, and that strengthened my resolve. I didn't have a clear plan of what I would do when I got to the restaurant, but I wasn't just about to sit around and do nothing.

"Maybe. I don't know but…" My voice trailed off. I wasn't sure what else to say. I was furious on Casey's behalf and felt I needed to do something. We had dealt with enough disrespect over the years, and this was the final straw. I might have fucked things up, but Casey was innocent. She didn't deserve this.

"You don't have to go there, Regina," Casey said finally. She looked up at me, eyes still shiny with unshed tears. The look on her face damn near broke my heart. "When he gets home—"

"If I let him get home," I interrupted. I reached out and covered her still-shaking hands with my own. "You stay here with the boys. I'm going to—"

"You can't kill him."

I sighed before pasting a soft smile on my face. "Of course, I can't. But I can remind him who he's messing with. You're the nice one, remember? Not me."

Casey gave me a watery smile. "You are nice."

"To you," I said with a snort. "I need to borrow a dress."

By the time I pulled up to the restaurant, I had half of a plan. I didn't think I would be able to get in and seated without Ray seeing me, but then again, going for the sneak attack wasn't really my thought process. I wanted him to see me, and I wanted to see his reaction to seeing me. When I walked into *Juliet's*, I had a moment of déjà vu. I had been to this place more than I liked in the past two weeks.

It was just as annoyingly charming as before, and I had to hand it to Jonathan, he had a gorgeous restaurant. Too bad his personality couldn't be as charming as his taste in dining. The hostess walked up, but I declined seating, instead making my way to the bar. I had sent the photo to my own phone, so I knew that Ray and his dinner companion were seated toward the back. From the bar, I should be able to get a few glances their way before he noticed me. I wanted to observe their body language first and get an idea what I was working with. If this really was a business dinner, I didn't want to cause problems for him and, by extension, Casey. I ordered a glass of wine and settled in to wait.

Chapter Five

Jonathan

"Mr. Dummond."

I looked up from my paperwork at Gregory's voice. He peeked his head in through the doorway, and I waved him in.

"I have the information you requested." He walked in with a thick folder clutched in his hands. "It took some digging, but I found the old files with information on the Mayfield Group and Dummond Enterprises' previous business dealings."

"Perfect," I replied, taking the offered folder. "I appreciate you compiling this for me, and I trust all of the information found will remain strictly between us."

Gregory nodded. "Of course, sir." I didn't doubt he would. Gregory had been my executive assistant for the past five years, and he had proven himself more than capable.

With a sharp nod, I dismissed him, smiling when he quickly made himself scarce. I appreciated his ability to give me the information I desired and keep it pushing. I made a note to myself to contact payroll to provide him a bonus on his next paycheck before turning my attention to the files. His husband's birthday was coming soon, so I know it would be appreciated. Plus, my own cursory search into my father's dealings with the Mayfields had yielded next to nothing that would give me a hint as to why Regina was keen on business with the Boldens. Even if it wasn't about her, my curiosity would have been piqued. It was why I had tasked Curtis with doing an audit of our client accounts beyond the norm and why I had others looking into my father specifically.

It shouldn't have taken so much digging to find information on a former business partner. From what little I remembered, the Mayfields had been involved in a few ventures, mostly in the food and hospitality sector. There shouldn't have been any reason to bury this information. Something wasn't adding up.

When I looked over the files, most of it was information I already knew. Regina's paternal grandfather had started with one diner in the forties and slowly built the business, adding two more locations before passing the helm down to his son, Regina's father. He'd done well in the seventies and eighties, turning their diners into a brand and expanding into new locales. It was impressive growth, and all projections had looked positive based on the information.

Not to mention, everything about the Mayfield Group's profile spoke to clean business and a penchant for altruism. The two men had been commendable, with both being lauded for giving back to the communities they served either through volunteering or supporting grassroots ventures. Hell, how they got involved with my father was anyone's guess. The Mayfield Group had steadily grown in revenue and prominence up until Regina's dad started associating with mine and, by default, Regina associating with me.

With a sigh, I leaned back against my chair. It was a tale as old as time in many ways. The Mayfields weren't the first or the last to go into business with my father and walk away worser for it, and it was compounded by the fact that I was probably part of the reason for it.

"How had I not known?"

The question hung in the air as I turned to stare out the window. Regina and I had grown up parallel to one another. We had attended the same private school, one that was no doubt recommended by my own father. It was high school when she and I started a friendship that turned into something more. It wasn't until college that shit had fallen apart and made our relationship one of many casualties.

I ran a hand over my face when I remembered my own part in that shit storm. I held no illusions that some of her anger was entirely my fault. I had still given a shit about what my father thought of me and my decisions, and he wasn't shy about sharing just what he thought about my relationship with his business partner's daughter. I could still hear the faint sounds of him yelling. Regina had clearly been aware of the issue, and I hadn't helped things by implying we should sneak around. My cheek still felt the phantom pain of the slap she had given me in response.

Still, I knew that couldn't have been the only reason things had soured so thoroughly. No, the complete and utter fuckery that ensued had my dad's fingerprints all over it. But one question still remained. Why?

I continued sifting through the documents until I came upon some that surprised me. They weren't about the Mayfields' business dealings but about Regina herself. Some of the information I knew. She and her parents had moved to London where her mother was from, though her older sister, Casey, had stayed behind with her now-husband. Regina had gone to college in London, then there were vague mentions of spending time in other parts of Europe, though there was no mention of why. I pulled out a couple pictures of her until one caught my eye.

She was clearly much younger. It might have even been taken right after they left the States. It was a simple picture of her in an airport. Her parents were standing a few feet from her, but my gaze was caught on Regina's expression and the tears on her cheeks. I swallowed hard at the thought of what must have put them there.

"Fuck," I whispered before dropping the folder onto my desk. Tears had never moved me before, so why were hers so fucking powerful? Seeing her so distraught even years ago did something to me that was fucking unforgivable.

It made me feel.

It was the same as when I had seen the fire blazing from her eyes as we stood face-to-face in that office. Anger. Rage. From most people, it rolled off my back. Their feelings were their own to deal with, and I felt no need to respond one way or another unless an imminent threat was near. But from her, there was no fear at seeing those emotions aimed at me, only excitement. I wanted that fire. Craved it now that I had gotten a single taste. The char of it still sat heavy and maddening on my tongue.

Past Regina had been soft-spoken with quiet smiles and a laugh that felt like the fluffiest hug. It had been so contrary to what I normally experienced that I couldn't help but be drawn to her. The Regina of now was the opposite of that softness, and yet, I found that as much as I had enjoyed the simple quiet of her personality when we were younger, I enjoyed the fiery woman she had been replaced with even more. I had more questions than ever and a burning need to get answers. My phone ringing caught my attention, and if not for who it was, I would've ignored the call completely.

"Jerome, what did you do now?"

"I resent the fact that every time I call one of you, you think I've done something."

"That's because usually when you call, you have done something. I'm not posting bail for you, so get someone else to do it."

I moved to hang up the phone, but his shout made me pause. "I'm not in jail, you asshole! But if you really want to be like that, then I won't tell you who just walked through the doors of *Juliet*'s."

With a growl of frustration, I put the phone on speaker. "Jerome, I swear—"

"So you don't want to know that Regina is here and looking *damn* fine?" I froze at his words. "Maybe I should go buy her a drink myself and see if she's as good in bed as the rumors say."

"What rumors?"

His chuckle had me gripping the phone tightly. "You are so out of the loop, big brother. I suggest you hightail it over here before someone else decides to shoot their shot."

I was halfway out of my chair before I realized it. Why was Regina back at my restaurant? Once could be chalked up to coincidence, but this was clearly something more. Regina knew it was my place and that I was often there. Was she trying to run into me? As self-centered of a thought as it was, it had me foolishly hoping that was the case. There was still the matter of her family and my family's bad blood. I knew I needed to be cautious with her, but everything in me screamed out that if she wanted to burn us, I would happily walk into the flames.

"Did she come with anyone?" I asked Jerome as I locked the folder away in my lockbox and prepared to leave. I looked down at the watch on my wrist and noted that, with the traffic, it shouldn't take me too long to get there.

"Looks like she came alone, but with the way she's looking, she definitely won't be leaving that way," he replied. "If you're coming, you better hurry up. I'll see what I can do to stall her or at least keep the vultures from circling. Let me know when you're here."

He hung up before I could reply, but there was nothing left for me to say. I quickly shut things down and made my way down to the car. Thankfully, the traffic decided to be kind and get the fuck out of my way, and twenty minutes later, I was making my way into *Juliet's*. Jerome met me at the doorway and gestured to the bar.

"She probably knows you're coming." He held up his hands when I gave him a look. "Hey, don't blame me. I didn't say anything about you, but she's observant, and I am the younger, hotter version of you."

He was right about her easily sniffing out when someone was overstepping, and I couldn't deny it. I doubted I had the element of surprise here. "Did she say why she's here?" Jerome shrugged and tucked his hands in his pockets. I frowned at his jeans. "And why are you coming into my restaurant dressed like that?"

He laughed. "They're called jeans, brother. I know for a fact you own some. And why is because they are comfortable."

I scowled. "I know what they are. We have a dress code."

"And I don't give a shit," he replied with a smile. "I suggest you spend less time worrying about what's covering my ass and think about how to cover your own when you walk in there. Regina looked like she was ready to throw all the hands, and I feel sorry for whoever it was that pissed in her cereal today. Good luck."

He gave me a salute before walking over to where the valet pulled up in his car. I stared at him for a moment longer before turning my attention to the restaurant. There was a commotion going on near the back, but I didn't see Regina anywhere. I walked over to the bar, wondering if maybe she had gone to the ladies' lounge. When I glanced to the back of the dining room, I finally caught a glimpse of her, along with a waitress who looked like she was about to shit herself. With a frown, I made my way over there.

"Is everything alright?"

The waitress turned to look at me, her eyes wide and more than a little afraid. I didn't recognize her, so I figured she was one of the new people hired in the last week or two. "Oh, Mr. Dummond, sir."

"Everything is fine, Jonathan," Regina said steely. She didn't bother glancing my way, instead continuing to glare down at the two people seated at the table. I didn't recognize the man, but I did recognize his dining companion.

"Elizabeth, it's good to see you again." I nodded at her before dismissing the waitress. "What seems to be the problem?"

Regina turned to me then, her hands crossed across her chest. "Jonathan, I'd like to introduce you to my brother-in-law, Raymond." She narrowed her eyes. "He's married to my *sister*, Casey."

I nodded before realizing exactly what it looked like. *Well, fuck.* Now I knew why Regina was so enraged. She had always been particularly protective of her older sister to the point that everyone knew it was the one subject not to touch. I could understand it. I'd bury anyone who fucked with one of my siblings. I gave them shit because I could. If anyone else tried it, they would find out just how I felt about that.

I stared, not knowing what to say. We were making a scene, and I wasn't looking forward to finding myself on one of those gossip accounts that made shit up for fun and got around the blatant falsehoods by claiming it was all for entertainment. "Perhaps we should take this conversation somewhere more private."

"That sounds like an excellent idea," Regina said, turning her gaze back to Elizabeth and Raymond. "Ray, you should probably take things somewhere much more private—like your home, where your wife is waiting for you."

That had me looking at the man, Raymond, in a new light. Clearly, he was in some sort of business. He had the sort of dress sense that screamed he was trying to make moves. Men like him were used to taking risks, but I wasn't sure if this was one he should take. Setting Regina off was not a good plan. I didn't know Casey well enough to know what was in store for him when he got home, but I could only hope he knew how to grovel.

"This was all very interesting, but I have zero desire in getting wrapped up in unnecessary drama." Elizabeth gathered her purse and stood. "Raymond, call me when things become a little more drama-free. It was good to see you again, Jonathan. We'll have to do lunch soon."

I nodded at her. She wasn't my type when it came to women, but her family and mine were friendly enough and had been for years. She was Liam Bolden's cousin, and though they were family, her dad was known for upstanding business and had never been known to play dirty. I actually admired the man and, before tonight, had never heard a bad word about Elizabeth. I wasn't sure what to make of this situation, so I decided to wait. Regina was running this show, and currently, I was just an observer.

Speaking of Regina, I was surprised when she stayed quiet as Elizabeth gathered her things and left. I would have thought she would let out a snide comment, but her gaze was surprisingly trained on Raymond, who was muttering apologies to Elizabeth. When she was out of earshot, he turned, a scowl painted on his face.

"What the fuck were you thinking?"

"I was thinking I should beat your ass and throw you face-first into Lake Lanier," Regina hissed. "The fuck were you thinking, wining and dining another fucking woman?"

Raymond glanced at me before turning his attention back to her. "It wasn't what it looked like, Regina. I told Casey tonight was a business meeting and that's what this was."

"Was it business when you were holding her goddamn hand?"

I raised my eyebrows at that. I hadn't been on hand to see anything happen, but if what she was saying was true, there was no way that could be explained away. Other than shaking hands, there was no reason to actually touch one another during a business meeting. It wasn't looking good for Raymond, and if Regina really wanted to get at him, I might let her get a couple licks in before stepping in.

"I wasn't holding her—"

Regina moved, and without a thought, I placed a hand on her shoulder. I wouldn't stop her if she really wanted to go after him, but I would rather it not be so public. Raymond seemed to realize he was this close to meeting God and closed his mouth with a click.

Regina was practically vibrating under my hand, and I worried things were about to get ugly really quick. Raymond didn't seem inclined to say more, which I wasn't sure would help or hinder him when it came to getting popped by the world's most overprotective sister. I decided to risk taking control of things.

I nodded to him and gently squeezed Regina's shoulder.

"I think we'd better take things to a more private location. There's an office around the corner that should be unoccupied."

"You put me in a room with him and only one of us is walking out," she replied, body still poised.

"I swear, Regina, I wasn't—"

"I don't want to hear it. Take your ass home," Regina cut in, voice coming out in a hiss. "Straight home. Do not stop. I know exactly how long it will take you to get there, and if I call and you aren't, I promise you Casey will be just fine with becoming a widow."

He narrowed his eyes. "You don't have a card to play here, Regina. This is my business you're messing with."

"When it involves my sister, it is my business," she countered. Her body was no longer vibrating. Now, every muscle seemed tense like a lioness poised to strike. Truthfully, I wanted to see exactly what she would do to him, given the chance. I held no love for cheaters, having dealt with that shit my whole life. "You're looking casket sharp right now, so I suggest you get the fuck out of my sight."

Raymond glanced at me before scowling. "You think you're hot shit because you have a Dummond on your side but remember who took your sister in when you fucked things up for her."

"I don't need Jonathan to make you another Lanier casualty. Keep playing with me," she spit out, sounding thoroughly disgusted. I was there myself. I knew this wasn't my battle, but from what I remembered, Casey was a nice person. I hadn't interacted with her a lot and didn't keep up with her once Regina left the country, but I couldn't remember anything egregious popping up about her.

"I think it's time for you to go," I said, pausing Raymond's comeback. I waved at the waitress, who had been politely hovering in the background. I didn't doubt she had heard everything, and I noted her name in case any of this information made it to the daily gossip rags. "Please escort Raymond to valet to collect his vehicle. You can charge this meal to my card. Consider it a gift." I raised an eyebrow at him.

He glared, gaze tracking back and forth between Regina and me before he finally seemed to give up and turned to follow the waitress.

I could feel the tension slowly dissipate, though I couldn't find it in me to move my hand from Regina's shoulder. I didn't doubt she was serious about her threats, but I hoped she would hold off. Hiding a body was far more difficult than it seemed, and I didn't think she was in any mood to do it without making a mistake.

"I bet you loved that."

"Loved what?"

She glanced over her shoulder at me. "Watching me lose control."

I frowned at her words. "Why would I have loved that?"

She stared for a moment before her gaze slowly drifted down to where I was still holding her shoulder. "Are you going to move your hand?"

I sighed and dropped it, forcing myself not to trail over the heat of her arm. "Are you going to answer any of my questions or continue countering with your own?"

"I wouldn't want to make things too easy for you," she replied, turning to face me fully. She crossed her arms, and I tried not to look at the way the move tightened the fabric of her dress. I knew she wouldn't appreciate being ogled while she was in a mood.

"Nothing about you is easy, Regina."

"The fuck is that supposed to mean?"

With a sigh, I wondered why I thought to say anything. Clearly, she had shit she needed to work out, and I cursed my old man for leaving me to deal with the brunt of it when it was more than likely his fault.

The small bit of information I had been able to read over before leaving the office sure as fuck seemed to lean in that direction.

"Does your animosity have to do with our fathers severing their business relationship?"

She gave me a narrow-eyed look. "You almost sound like you really don't know what happened."

"That's because I don't."

"I find that hard to believe."

I shrugged. "You can find it however you'd like, but it's the truth. The old man wasn't exactly forthcoming when it came to shit. The two of you have that in common."

Her hands balled into fists, and I knew it was a low blow, but damnit, I was tired of being the last one to know what the fuck was going on. I was dealing with that shit enough at work, I wasn't about to deal with it in my personal life too. And regardless of what Regina said, it was the goddamn truth.

"You and yours packed up and left with no heads-up. And I get it, I fucked up when I asked you to keep our relationship quiet."

"Quiet?" she said, jerking toward me before she caught herself. I held my ground before deciding this conversation didn't need to be broadcast to the rest of the patrons. I thought for sure she would take a swipe at me when I cupped her elbow and considered it a win when she went willingly with me to the hallway leading to the offices and lounges.

"Yes, quiet," I repeated before letting go of her elbow. "I get it was unfair of me to ask you—"

"Unfair is putting it far too mildly," she said, cutting off my words. "You wanted me to stay quiet and be your little side bitch while you married some fucking Stepford wife."

I ran a hand over my face. This conversation was not going how I had hoped, but I knew some shit needed to be aired out. "You're right. I should never have asked something like that of you." Regina's expression didn't change, but I continued. "I'm sorry for not standing up for what we had then. I was so caught up in being exactly the type of man my father wanted that I hurt you."

"You were a coward," she spit out, though I could hear the hurt in her voice. "You hurt me, and then you let your father twist the goddamn knife in."

"Regina, you're right. I hurt you. But I'm standing here telling you that's all I know. I'm asking you to explain to me what happened."

"Your father–"

"My father is dead," I said flatly. "I loved the man because he was my father, but good fucking riddance."

Regina's expression slowly morphed into something less harsh and more confused than anything. "You worshipped your father. You wanted to be just like him."

I sighed and scrubbed a hand over my face. "Yes, I did then. But then I got to know him. The real him, and I simply did what I had to do to keep my family together and my siblings out of the worst of it. I chose the lesser of two fucking evils, Regina."

Those words hurt. Fuck, did they ever hurt. But they were the fucking truth. I knew it, my siblings knew it. Hell, our mother knew it, and that was probably why she had gone MIA. Jonathan Sr. might have been a great businessman, but he was a shit father and, from the rumors, an even worse husband.

I wanted nothing more than to be different.

Chapter Six

Regina

I stared hard at Jonathan, waiting to see if he would crack. I didn't know if he was trying to play me for a fool, but I couldn't deny that it was starting to seem like he was sincere. His confusion was starting to piss me off even more. How dare he not know what happened after I spent ten years of my life planning to get back at him and his fucking family? Was I wrong about what had happened? Everything pointed toward no, yet there were clearly some unanswered questions.

I didn't like unanswered questions. When it came to deciding on my next steps, pulling the trigger with incomplete information wouldn't be wise. I crossed my arms again, hoping to radiate annoyance and not the confusion swirling in my mind. I couldn't have him thinking I was wavering on my stance of hating him.

"Are you seriously telling me you don't know what your father did?" I asked flatly. I didn't want to give anything away, but I needed to get a complete picture of what Jonathan knew. His father had not been someone who would willingly admit to being in the dark about anything even if it were clear he was unaware. The small part of me that wanted to believe Jonathan was telling the truth needed to know if he was just like his father. If he was, he would go down along with the others. I wasn't trying to be merciful, but I needed to understand.

"Honestly, look me in the face and tell me you didn't know what your father did."

Dark brown eyes looked horrifyingly sincere. "I have no idea what he did to your family, Regina. That's the truth." He opened his hands as if in supplication. I wanted to slap at them, but I kept the desire to myself and let him continue talking. "I know that after you and I ended, our fathers fell out with one another, and I know mine probably used that as justification for whatever the fuck he did, like always."

"Do you really think anything could justify trying to bankrupt the company my family worked so hard to build?" I asked, not caring if my voice raised and others heard. We were talking about my family, my legacy here, and I refused to back down.

"No," he replied, shaking his head. "I'm not saying that at all. Is that what happened?"

I looked him up and down, wondering if he were playing coy with his knowledge. "You really didn't know?"

"I have no reason to lie to you, Regina," Jonathan said. "I tried asking my father about what happened once. He acted like he didn't know what I was talking about and then berated me about some shit that had nothing to do with me. You know how he was."

I did know how he was, and I begrudgingly acknowledged that if Jonathan Sr. didn't want to talk, nothing and no one could get him to. I remembered my mom and dad talking about his stubborn streak that was accompanied by his mean streak.

When someone walked past us on the way to the lounge, I realized the hallway was probably not the best place to be having this conversation. "You mentioned there being an office?"

Jonathan slowly nodded before glancing around. "Same one as last time."

I swallowed hard as I remembered just which office he meant. Despite how hard I tried, the memories of his body against mine hadn't been far from my thoughts. It was becoming a real problem. "Right. Maybe we should continue this conversation there."

He looked at me for a moment, gaze heavy and filled with some unnamed emotion.

"Probably for the best." He gestured for me to walk past, and I took the opening.

The heat of him pushed me forward as I turned down a familiar hallway. When we reached a door, a hand gently dropped against my back.

"No need to knock. I saw the manager at the front of the dining room as we walked over."

I nodded before turning the knob and letting us in. The office looked the same as before, with a couple of filing cabinets on the far wall and a large desk to the right. It wasn't the largest, but then again, I supposed it didn't need to be.

When the snick of the door closing behind us reached me, I slowly turned. Now that we were alone together again, it felt like Jonathan's presence filled the small room. I tried not to show that I was affected. There was no fear. There was something even worse….appreciation.

I appreciated the way his broad shoulders filled out his suit jacket and the way the cut seemed tailored to show off his waist. My gaze was even more appreciative of the long legs accentuated by well-tailored slacks. Yes, there was a lot to appreciate about Jonathan. It pissed me the fuck off. I wished he was ugly. It would have made things so much easier.

"Do you believe me now?" he asked, pulling my attention back up to his face. I raised an eyebrow to cover up the fact I had been admiring him instead of being angry.

"Maybe," I replied, not wanting to give too much too soon. "Aren't you the head bastard in charge now? How wouldn't you have known about past business relationships?"

"I'm trying to understand that myself," he said, showing the first bit of emotion. "Each day I'm learning more and more that I don't like."

That surprised me. I would've thought for sure being the one tapped to take over that Jonathan would know everything that had happened. It didn't make any sense he would be kept in the dark about matters that could affect the running of his family's numerous business ventures once he took it over. Then again, I'd heard his dad had died of a heart attack. No one could have planned for that even if they tried. Maybe it meant he wasn't fully prepared to hand things over. That did change things a bit, and I would need to rethink my strategy.

"So, let's say I believe you," I said after a moment of silence. "Let's say you really had no idea why our families fell out. That still doesn't change the fact that your family took everything from mine. Clients stopped doing business with us because of it. We had to close up nearly every restaurant from here to Toronto just to salvage things until the company recovered."

"And I'm sorry for that," he replied. "I'd like to think that if I had known, I would have pushed back against him regardless of the consequences."

As much as I wanted to call bullshit, the same small part of me that wanted to believe could appreciate his honesty. It didn't change my plans, but I would give him that much.

"Really?" The question was out before I could think about how it would look. The strangely hopeful tone of my voice had me wincing internally.

What the fuck did it matter if he would have tried to stop his dad? I doubt it would have changed anything.

Jonathan took a step forward.

"Of course. I had hoped that eventually, we would come clean about our relationship."

I snorted. "Relationship? Is that what we had?" I felt the spark of my anger ignite, and I appreciated it. Clung to it in the face of this new, strangely beseeching Jonathan. "What happened to us not tying things down with labels?"

Jonathan sighed. "Regina."

"No." I let my irritation grow. "You were the one who refused to tell your father you were fucking a commoner.

You don't get to rewrite history just because the man is dead. That doesn't change things, Jonathan."

"I know that," he countered. "I know I fucked up then. I didn't know how to bring it up, so I took the easy way out. After you left, the fact that I never got to apologize ate me up inside, but I figured you didn't want to speak to me."

"At least you got one thing right."

"What would you have me do?" he asked. "I can't change the past, so what can I do to get you to forgive me?"

I slowly dropped my arms as I stared. That was not a question I was expecting to get from him.

"I want what was taken from me. With interest." He frowned and cocked his head. I bit the inside of my cheek and refused to find the move cute.

"Done. How much do you need?"

I blinked slowly. What was he playing at? Did he really think it was that simple to make things better? To make things right? In a split decision, I decided to go for it all.

"There were business decisions that impacted our company's growth for the last ten years. I know you're loaded along with the business, but are you really capable of giving back everything?"

He paused then, and a sick feeling of glee enveloped me. I knew I was correct. There was no way in hell he was able to give back what his family had stolen. "Then, if you're really serious, sign your restaurants over to me and we'll call it even."

"You know that's not possible."

I shrugged, wanting to seem nonchalant. "You were the one who said you could replace what your family stole. So, if you're saying you can't, then get out of my way."

I moved to go past him, but a hand on my arm stopped me. I tried not to think about the heat of it, the way it leached into my skin and seemed to call to the knot of emotions that burned in my chest.

"Move."

He moved, but to further block my exit. I balled my fists, not wanting to resort to violence but not discounting the potential need for it. I wasn't delusional. If Jonathan wanted to hurt me, he probably could, but I was going to make sure I got my licks in before that happened. I had never known him to be violent. Then again, with his family's money and connections, even if he were, I probably would never hear about it except for whispered gossip that no one would ever cop to. If I had known what was about to come out of his mouth, I probably would've hit him.

"Marry me."

Chapter Seven

Jonathan

I wasn't sure what was going to come out of my
mouth until the words were already out there, sitting in the
air like stale humidity. Impulsivity wasn't the norm for me,
but there was no way to take the words back now that they
had been given voice. The strangest part was I didn't want
to. While Regina had been talking, a plan slowly formed in
my head. I knew there was no way in hell she would
consider my proposal on a normal day. But today was not a
normal day, and ours was not a normal relationship. The
time for normalcy was ten years ago when I fucked things
up following my bastard of a father's wishes. If he were
alive and privy to my thoughts, he'd probably be screaming.
But he was dead, and I didn't give a fuck about what he

thought anymore. I wanted Regina, and I would do anything to have her back at my side.

"What did you just say?" she asked, her voice gone shrill. I stepped forward and reached out, taking a chance that maybe in her surprise, she wouldn't try to rip my arm off. When I placed a hand on her shoulder, she looked at it but otherwise did nothing. I couldn't help but run my thumb over the skin of her collarbone.

"Marry me."

"Did you hit your head on the way over here?" she asked. "Should I call someone? Do you need a therapist?"

I snorted. "Probably." Tonight, I was clearly all about taking risks because I moved closer and let my hand slide down her arm to curl around her wrist. "You want to build your family's company back. Marry me, and I will give you the resources you need to do so."

She looked down at my hand before looking back up at me. "And if I planned on taking down your father's company and embarrassing you all publicly?"

"I don't think any of my siblings nor I possess a single ounce of shame," I replied. "Jameson would probably shit himself laughing, to be honest. He struck out on his own for a reason."

"And you?" she asked, cocking her head as she looked at me. "You would be okay with me pushing for the downfall of your father's legacy?"

"Even without Dummond Enterprises, my siblings and I are set up very well," I answered truthfully. I wasn't boasting but letting her know the reality of the situation. As much as the company was our father's legacy, it still came with bittersweet feelings. If not for his death, I doubted all of us would still be working in the family business within the next five years. Jameson had started something that had slowly begun to take hold in the rest of us. Thoughts of something *more*.

"Money earned can always be lost."

I nodded at Regina's words. She was right, of course. You heard all the time of people who suddenly came into money only to squander it away a scant few years later. "I can't believe you asked me to marry you. Who fucking does that?"

I chuckled. "Me, apparently. And yet, you still haven't answered me."

"I heard the words you said, I just don't understand why you thought they needed to be. Why the hell would I marry you?"

I brushed my thumb over the back of her hand as I tried to think of the words that would put this all into perspective. This plan of mine was only half-formed, but I was good at thinking on my feet, and when it came to Regina, that was something I was going to have to get used to. No one had challenged me like her, and while on one hand, I hated it—hated it with a fiery passion that burned deep in my soul—on the other, I craved it.

The few women our parents had tried to set me up with had only been into it for the status. They had been more than happy to step back and do nothing but lap up what the name would bring. That kind of relationship might have been fine for some, but the more I saw of Jameson and McKenzie, how their strengths and weaknesses ebbed and flowed together, the more I longed for something similar. I needed that push and pull of personalities to see the world in color. Most people were gray, dull and uninspired. But Regina was something different. Even before now, she had always been there in technicolor on the edge of my senses.

"Say yes."

"You're being absurd."

I nodded. "Maybe. But all great businessmen take risks." I took one then and pulled her closer to me. She put up the barest amount of resistance before I once again had her in my arms. "I have questions, you have answers. I have money, you want success."

She rolled her eyes. "Right. We're a match made in heaven."

"Heaven. Hell. Two sides of the same coin." I stared down into her dark brown eyes and felt myself getting lost in them. "Say yes."

She clenched her jaw before looking away. "I need to think about it."

"One week," I replied, slowly loosening my hold on her waist. "Get your plans in order. I'll reserve us a table at *Bones*. Have your answer ready then."

Regina's eyes narrowed, and I expected more of a fight, but she nodded sharply before pulling away. I stepped away from the door, letting her leave. She wasn't the only one who needed to get prepared. I had a folder to look through and a long talk to have with myself to figure out if I had just signed away my soul.

~*~*~

It had been a long week. My concentration had been utter shit, and I'd had to excuse myself from a few meetings just to schedule emergency personal trainings that would exhaust my body and my mind. All I could think about were those two little words and the fact that I had given Regina the key to my potential ruin. I had done more digging of my own with some of my contacts and had been surprised to see Regina still courting Liam Bolden and his family's connections. That was something that needed to be nipped in the bud. It wouldn't do for Regina to be associated with slimy business, especially given the Boldens didn't try all that hard to hide it. Father used to say they had more money than sense, and I believed it.

Jameson had questioned my disappearing acts but hadn't pried too hard. I knew he probably thought I was having some late onset grief about our father, but truthfully, I was trying to figure out the rules of engagement I was going to set before Regina when we met for dinner. *If we met.* There was a small, worried voice inside of me that wondered if she would even bother to show up tonight. I didn't even have her number so I couldn't call her to confirm. Well, truthfully, I had gotten her number from my searches, but I was trying my best not to overstep. I knew she wouldn't appreciate my less-than-normal advances. It was why I was now seated at the table and hoping beyond odds that she decided to show.

Movement at the curtain caught my eye. The relief I felt was palpable when I saw Regina step around it, and I quickly stood. Her eyes found me almost immediately, and I sucked in a deep breath as I looked her up and down.

Red was her color. Hell, every color was her color, but there was something special about seeing her decked out in a hue as bold as the personality beneath it that had my ass sitting up straight and taking notice. There was a confidence there that I had only seen glimpses of years ago when the weight of my last name had been enough to rip apart what little innocence I'd ever had. I wondered what it had taken to pull that confidence to the forefront. I could almost taste the bite of lightning on the back of my tongue. Playing with Regina was dangerous, if not for my legacy, then definitely for my soul.

This feeling, the rush of heat and sharp want was familiar, though I hadn't felt it in years. At least, not to this level. This was damn near thought-obliterating as I watched Regina saunter slowly toward me. I could almost feel the change in the air with each step she took, and I only had to glance around to know I wasn't the only one who noticed her. Curves in all the right fucking places drew admiring eyes and the tight red material of her dress only put them on starker display. When she was finally in front of me, I clenched my fists to keep from reaching out with the desperate need to touch what wasn't mine.

Yet.

"Meeting in public?" she asked with an arch of her brow. "Were you afraid I might harm you in some way?"

The thought of her getting violent hadn't crossed my mind when I asked her to meet me here, but I knew there were plenty of ways to end someone that didn't require physical touch. No, I was more worried about myself being alone with her. Anyone else and I wouldn't have been the slightest bit concerned. Then again, no one had ever gotten under my fucking skin like her. Regina was in a class of her own, and everything in me had always taken notice. That hadn't changed, regardless of our years apart. Still, I knew the game, and I knew I had to play it carefully.

"No," I answered simply before pulling the chair out for her. "I just figured conversation would flow easier if we were in neutral territory."

Regina's dark eyes assessed me, moving up and down as if scanning every inch, and I swallowed hard, trying not to appear affected. The ball was in her court right now. If she turned and walked away, I would have no choice but to turn and give chase. I couldn't ignore my own sense of relief when instead, she sat gingerly in the offered chair. I pushed it closer to the table and moved around to sit back in my own seat. The waiter placed down menus, and I ordered a bottle of Château Cheval Blanc before allowing my gaze to drift back across the table.

Chatter from the front faded to the background and the light was muted, setting a mood that called for softer voices and an intimacy that had me wanting to reach across the table to pull Regina to my side. Despite what some might say, I didn't have a death wish, so I kept my hands to myself.

The scent of her was almost overwhelming, and I had to stop myself from leaning in to take in more. It was damn near impossible to look at anything else but her.

"You're staring," she said softly. I smiled when she looked up at me from beneath kohl-dark eyelashes. "Do you have something you would like to share with the class?"

"That depends."

"On what?"

I picked up the menu and opened it. "On what your answer is."

Regina snorted. "That sounds like blackmail. I thought you weren't into playing dirty."

I raised an eyebrow and smirked. "I don't do dirty business. When it comes to my social life, however, the dirtier the better."

"Is that so?" she asked before glancing down at the menu. She ran her finger over the edge of it, and I was helpless not to follow the motion. "From what I've heard, you don't play much of anything. Word on the street is you're a perpetual bachelor who doesn't have a sex drive at all."

That was a new one. "Who the hell did you hear that from?" I asked, wondering just who I needed to hunt down. "There's a difference between not having sex and being discreet about it."

"Never implied otherwise," she said before leaning back. The waiter returned with our wine, and once the glasses were poured, I attempted to get to the bottom of such a ridiculous rumor.

"I can't believe you thought I was celibate."

Regina swirled the wine in her glass before taking a sip. "I never thought anything that had to do with you and sex. I was only informing you of what people were saying. If it were me, I would want to know."

I snorted but paused to take my own sip. "Well, thank you for letting me know. I suppose next time I'll make sure my partner does the walk of shame to prove my prowess between the sheets."

"I thought you wanted me to marry you?" she countered, glancing at me over the rim of her glass. "Or are you actually the type to marry and have a mistress on the side?"

Following these accusations was a lot like playing tennis. As soon as you hit the ball, it would be smacked right back to you. So, what did it say about me that I was enjoying it?

"If you had asked me years ago, I probably would have agreed that's the way it would be." Regina narrowed her eyes, but I remained calm. I didn't see any point in starting this thing between us with a lie. It was a well-known secret that a lot of successful men married for one reason and kept a lover for another.

Discretion was the name of the game and one I might have played before I knew better.

"So, you were serious back then when you asked me to keep things quiet," she replied. "So, what? You planned to keep me on the side while you married some other girl with better breeding than me?"

I thought for a moment of how I could phrase things to not get my head chewed off. If it were anyone else, I would have just said yes without a second thought. But fuck, Regina was different. I had to choose my words carefully if I wanted things to go my way.

"At one point in time, I worshipped my father," I began. "He was the person I looked up to the most in this world, and I thought he had all the answers to how life was supposed to be."

My words evoked the deep-down pain I kept hidden from my siblings and mother. At one point in time, I'm sure we all felt that way about him. When things were good, father had almost seemed larger than fucking life. He'd had that swagger about him that made people stop what they were doing and take notice. It had been almost like a show to watch as he worked his way through a crowd, drawing them in and leaving them waiting for more. It had been a style I was ill-equipped to copy. If anyone, Jameson fit the bill the most, and I had envied him for that. As the firstborn, I was supposed to be the mirror image to our father, and yet…

"But when I saw him for who he was, that all changed." I lifted my glass and stared at the dark liquid like it could make sense of these complicated feelings. "I would have done whatever he asked of me then, but I was a child. Foolish. Enamored with the power that came from our name."

"So you would have hurt me," she asked again, and this time, I gave her the answer she sought.

"Yes."

It was damning and freeing all at once. The knowledge was out there, bare for both her and me to see. It fell against the table like a boulder bearing down the hillside. There was no going back, but I could only hope the way forward was built on a stronger base.

"But that was then," I continued, looking up at her. Regina's face gave nothing away. I couldn't tell if she was angered by my admission. "Now, I would give you the world for another chance."

She looked down at the table as if seeing a scene for her eyes only. "I planned to ruin you. Just because you are being honest with me now doesn't mean my plans have changed. I will use you to get what I want."

I huffed out a soft laugh before raising my glass to her. "I would expect no less." I waited for her to make a move. Her gaze was steady as she stared at me. I let her look her fill, not bothering to hide just how much I wanted her to give in.

After what seemed like an eternity, Regina raised her wine glass. "You're a fool, Jonathan."

The sound of glass clinking resonated, and I knew then there was no turning back.

Chapter Eight

Regina

"Shit," I huffed out, nearly throwing my phone in anger. Taking a deep breath helped settle me slightly, but it did nothing for my racing thoughts. Damn my impulsivity. I had been thinking of nothing but Casey when I confronted Ray at the restaurant, and that was my first mistake. The second was not taking a look at the woman he was with and checking to see if I could find any information on her. If I had, I might have realized she was Liam's cousin, and then I might not be in this mess.

I crossed and recrossed my legs. Cracking my neck did little to release the tension, but I needed a moment of calm before rereading the message on my phone.

Unfortunately, after further discussion, we are unable to partner with you on the rebuild. Perhaps in the future, once you have proven your track record for growth, we can re-evaluate whether a partnership would be in both our best interests.'

Bastard. I knew exactly why he was pulling the plug, and I had no one to blame but myself. Casey being hurt was a soft spot for me and clearly, the distance between us hadn't lessened that fact. If not for the fact that Casey probably wouldn't approve, I would have put Ray in the ground a week ago. As it was, I hadn't talked to either one of them since that night. Casey had sent a text message when I was on my way home asking for space, and I had happily agreed. I knew she needed time, and as hard as it was to sit back and do nothing, I would follow her lead.

Then there was Jonathan's proposal. Literally, a fucking proposal. And for some fucked-up reason, I had agreed. To marriage. With him. I didn't know who was more delusional right now, me or him. I looked back down at the text message from Liam. I couldn't deny that Jonathan's proposal had come at just the right time. I could leverage my fictitious relationship with him to achieve just as much if not more than what I had hoped to with Liam. Hell, I probably could swing things to even knock him down a peg or two for shits and giggles.

"Fuck," I said aloud before leaning back in my chair. One corner of the ceiling had a water stain, and I frowned at the reminder that this place was not up to the standards I wanted to be in.

The office I was renting was small, with just enough room for my desk and a few storage cabinets. It was a far cry from the space I remembered visiting as a kid when my dad had his main base of operations in Atlanta. I had driven by the old building as soon as I got back, but it had already been torn down in favor of some new high-rise. The neighborhood around it had also been hit by the ongoing wave of gentrification, making it damn near unrecognizable.

A knock on my door had me pausing the downward spiral of my thoughts, and I looked up in time to see it open. I tossed my phone onto my desk, not caring where it landed at this point. I didn't want anything to do with the damn thing until I could plan out my next steps.

"I knew I heard someone breathing hard in here." Pasting a smile onto my face took some effort, but by the time Christa walked in, I had fixed my posture and looked less like I was ready to either strangle someone or collapse into tears.

"Christa, so good to see you." Really, having her here now was horribly inconvenient, but she didn't need to know that. I had already fucked things up with Liam, I couldn't afford to fuck up with her too. I stood and walked around my desk. "I'm glad you could meet me for lunch today."

Christa hugged me gently, and a cloud of nose-tingling perfume swept over me. I knew I would have to keep my door open for the rest of the day to air out my office, otherwise I would be sitting on a migraine come time to leave.

"Of course," she gushed, holding onto my shoulders. "When I heard you and Liam had a row, I figured you might need some cheering up."

I had to force myself not to snort in amusement. Was that the story he was going with? That he and I had a fight? I suppose it was better than him telling people I nearly had a moment where I ripped his cousin's head off. I doubted that would endear me to anyone who had the money and connections I needed to get what I wanted.

"Thank you so much," I replied, putting a slight whine in my voice to play things up.

I could see Christa's pity, and it made me want to vomit. Liam wasn't worth being sad over, but I knew that also wouldn't be the right angle to play. These men needed to feel like they were the high-value prize. Stroking egos was an Olympic sport in these circles and unfortunately, you had to play to win big. I would never settle for anything less than gold.

"I wish I had been able to introduce you to Elizabeth so you would have recognized her." Christa sat primly in the chair in front of my desk. I walked back to my own seat and sat down. "I heard it was quite the commotion until Jonathan showed up?"

I swallowed hard at his name being brought up. His presence was probably the only thing that kept me from going to jail that night, but it still pissed me off. The calm exterior I had built up abroad seemed to chip away each time he came around, and I didn't like it. I wasn't normally this impulsive person doing things without rhyme or reason. Every time I looked at myself in the mirror these days, I didn't recognize the woman staring back at me.

Pushing through the discomfort, I nodded with a contrite look on my face. "I was just so upset. You know, my sister has two kids, and they've been trying for a third. It's just been so upsetting to watch her go through this."

"Oh, honey," Christa cooed, making me want to choke. "I can only imagine."

"Jonathan was such an amazing help, though," I continued, trying to figure out how to bring up the agreement between us without raising any red flags. Despite the fact that arranging marriages was a normal thing in these circles, it was also something that wasn't talked about. You weren't supposed to act like you knew the relationships were arranged. No, to the outside, they were supposed to seem completely normal and not manufactured.

"Speaking of Jonathan…" Christa said. My heart started beating faster when her look turned sly, and I knew what she was planning to say. Gossip traveled fast, especially when you were seen having dinner with one of the richest and most well-connected. I hadn't said anything to anyone about my agreement with Jonathan. The one person I would have shared the information with was still incognito, and it wasn't the kind of information you would just text someone. That was a conversation for face-to-face communication so Casey could berate me for doing something so ridiculous, then swear herself to secrecy anyway. It was how things usually went between the two of us—her telling me I was ridiculous for even considering something and then supporting me regardless. If she had been the one interested in taking over the business, I'm sure we wouldn't even be in this mess.

"A little birdie told me they saw the two of you having a very cozy-looking dinner a couple nights ago."

I smiled demurely. Looking too pleased about the information leak would have raised suspicions. I needed to play things quietly for the next few weeks so I wouldn't seem too eager to wave around my relationship, no matter how fake.

"We were just having dinner and catching up," I replied. "We were friends a long time ago."

"I heard you might have been more than that," Christa said, leaning forward. She pitched her voice low as if she were afraid of someone else overhearing our conversation. There were a few other offices rented out on my floor, but for the most part, they seemed to be occupied by people who had even fewer visitors than me. I rarely heard anything louder than a soft murmur of voices, and even then, usually only when I had just gotten in or was about to leave for the day.

Jonathan and I hadn't talked about it, but we needed to meet up in order to get our stories straight. It wouldn't do for me to say one thing about how we met in our previous relationship and him to say something completely different. That would not only sow discord but also lead to more questions, more gossip, more tongues wagging. And that wasn't something I needed at this stage of the game. I didn't mind if people saw me and wondered where I came from, especially when they found out we were engaged. What I didn't want was people to start rumors about me coming in with ulterior motives. They would be correct, of course, but they didn't need to know that.

I stood and started gathering my things to give myself some time to think. I needed to keep the story as close to the truth as possible, especially since some of the information could be easily verified by talking to the right people.

"So, should we head to lunch?"

Christa stood but gave me a grin. "Oh? Are we changing the subject now?"

I shook my head. "I'm not changing the subject. But gossiping on an empty stomach is no fun at all," I replied, giggling softly before gesturing for her to follow me out of the office. I was grateful we were taking separate cars because it gave me time to call Jonathan.

"Regina."

"We have a problem."

I could hear voices talking in the background, and for a second, I felt bad about potentially interrupting him. Then again, he was the one who caused all this by being every-damn-where. A small part of me wondered if maybe he had planned the whole Ray thing too. Could he be that fucking devious?

If we were talking about his dad, I would have no problem believing it. But the part of me that still thought back to better days before reality washed everything in shades of gray wanted to trust he wouldn't fuck up my sister's life like that.

"One moment," Jonathan replied. I glanced at the cars around me before switching lanes. The talking in the background of the call grew fainter. "Alright. What's the problem?"

"Did I interrupt something?"

"Yes." I waited for him to say more, and when he didn't, I snorted in amusement.

"Okay. Well, like I said, we have a problem." I paused for a moment as I turned a corner. "I'm getting lunch with Christa, and apparently, last night we were spotted out."

Jonathan hummed, the rumble coming softly over the line and making me swallow hard. Those kinds of noises were unnecessary, and I needed him to stop. "We were out in public. It's inevitable that people would talk about seeing us together."

"Yes, but we don't need those people starting rumors before we've had time to come up with a story."

"I fail to see the problem," he replied, voice going flat. The sound of it reminded me so much of his father's indifference that it had me clenching my teeth. "What random people gossip about is none of my concern."

"Well, it is a concern of mine," I hissed back. Only the fact that I was behind the wheel kept me from going off. For someone who was supposedly a business genius, Jonathan was clearly inept at anything having to do with playing the social game. How the fuck had he gone through life not knowing that the people he shared spaces with thought he was a non-sexual Ken doll? Did he really not care? It must be nice to be able to win at life by doing the bare fucking minimum. It didn't work like that for me, and part of that was because of him. I had no desire to leave my life and future success in his hands when he clearly didn't know what the fuck to do with it.

"People will say what they want to say," he said in a tone bordering on condescending. "If you get caught up—"

"I don't need a lecture from you on self-esteem," I replied, cutting him off. "You've never had a damn thing to lose, and it shows by how little you've thought this out. And despite your insistence, I can see you don't give a shit about how this will affect me."

I jerked to a stop in front of the valet. Today was already going to shit, and it was only lunchtime.

"Regina, there's no need to be upset."

"I'm not upset, Jonathan. I'm disappointed. Disappointed that for a fleeting moment, I thought maybe you were different."

Before he could say anything else, I disconnected the call. Clearly, I needed to come at things from a different angle. I don't know why I thought I could rely on Jonathan, but I was thankfully dissuaded from that notion. I wouldn't make the same mistake again.

I pasted a smile on for the valet as he opened the door. Christa was already making her way inside, and when I stepped closer, she wrapped an arm in mine.

"I saw you chatting when you drove up. Were you talking to Jonnie?"

"I didn't realize anyone still called him that," I replied as we were led to our table. Once we were seated and had ordered drinks, I spoke again. "But yes, I was talking to him. Well, arguing more than anything. He can be so stubborn."

Christa giggled. "Aren't most men? Sometimes I think Marcello says no just because he can."

I nodded. He sounded like a few of the men I'd casually dated over the years. I didn't mind getting advice, particularly if someone had more experience or expertise than me, but I wasn't about to follow it just because someone had a dick.

With thirty dollars and an Amazon account, I could strap on a dick too. Hell, it would probably be more satisfying.

"But tell me more about this rekindled flame."

"I don't know about all that," I choked out before taking a sip of my drink. It didn't matter how I protested, Christa didn't seem to believe any of it. With a sigh, I figured I might as well give her something to spread around. A little breadcrumb. Nothing too major. "It was just dinner."

Her eyes lit up, and she leaned closer.

"No dessert?" She wiggled her eyebrows, and I found myself huffing out an amused laugh.

"Absolutely not," I confirmed. "What kind of girl do you take me for?"

She shrugged. "Liam was always going on about the dinners you two had. Did anything ever—"

"I never slept with Liam." I was firm in my words. That was not a rumor I wanted floating around with anyone. "He hinted a few times, but I have a firm rule of not mixing business with pleasure. I know you were hoping something different."

Christa waved off my words. "Truthfully, I didn't see you two getting serious. He's such a playboy."

"Didn't you try to set us up?"

"Only because I knew you needed an in." That was surprising. "Plus, I got so tired of his sister talking about how their mom wanted him to settle down with a nice girl. Nice girls do not go for him."

I laughed now and gave Christa a second look. Perhaps I had judged her too quickly. She had been born with a silver spoon in her mouth, which clearly showed in how she talked about the world around her, but overall, she seemed harmless. Plus, I needed to not be a hypocrite. I had told Jonathan he didn't know how to be around people socially. It wouldn't do for me to have the same problems.

Lunch went smoothly after that, with Christa divulging a little more information about Liam and his family as well as catching me up on the gossip going around. By the time my phone buzzed, letting me know I needed to get back to the office, we had already planned another lunch and dinner over the weekend. I was still wary, but I didn't think Christa was playing me. Hell, she seemed just as excited.

I waved down our waiter.

"Could we get the check, please?"

"Oh, your table has already been taken care of by a Mr. Dummond."

Christa's eyebrows raised, and she gave me a wide smile. "Well, that was nice of him."

I sighed internally as the waiter scurried away. *Damn it, Jonathan. What game are you playing at?*

Chapter Nine

Jonathan

This wasn't the first time I had called my siblings to a family dinner, but it was the first time I had something about me to say. I still wasn't able to reach our mother, but with Jameson's assurance that whoever he had tailing her said she was fine, I let her be. She was a major concern, but she was also an adult. If she wanted alone time after having saved face and kept mum on her thoughts for the past thirty-plus years, I would give that to her. It had taken some convincing for the others minus Jameson to feel the same. I knew Jalissa was feeling the most hurt, regardless of how she tried to hide it. Now that I had her across the table from me, I could see the strain. Still, I didn't have any assurances for her that mother would want to talk tomorrow or next week or even next month.

"So, what was the reason you pulled us back to this hellhole?" Jerome asked, breaking the silence that had fallen since the last dish had been served.

"You live here," Jameson said between bites.

"Doesn't mean I want to spend my every waking moment here," Jerome cut back. "Besides, I'm moving out next week. Remember?"

"It's about time you learned how to live on your own and clean up after yourself."

I sighed, knowing where this was headed. All of us had been pleasantly surprised when Jerome talked about finally striking out and getting a place of his own. Or rather, actually living on his own. He had his own portfolio of properties just like the rest of us, but he'd never lived in any of them, instead renting them out.

"Fuck you, Jimmy."

"Real original. Did mom help you write that one?"

"Can y'all shut the fuck up?" Jalissa hissed. I tried to hide my smirk when Jameson and Jerome went quiet. When she cut her eyes at me, I raised a brow. "Are you going to tell us why we're here or what? I have other places to be."

"And other people to be with," Jerome said under his breath.

When she cut her eyes to him, he held up his hands in surrender. I wasn't sure what that little dig was about, but I didn't push. I had my own agenda for the evening that didn't include whatever tiff she and Valerie had fallen into now.

"Right," I began. I set my fork down and turned to look at each of them steadily in turn. "Regina is back." Other than a couple of raised brows, none of them said anything. "And she asked me to sign over a few of our subsidiaries to her."

That did get a reaction.

"What the fuck? Why does she think you'd give her anything?" Jameson asked. "Is she pregnant or something?"

Jennifer snorted. "I thought for sure Jameson would knock someone up before you."

"Cute, Jen."

"I mean, she's not wrong," Jalissa chimed in.

"Who is Regina?" Jerome asked. It was a fair question, and the only reaction I deigned to reply to. He had been much younger when Regina and I were together, so I doubted he knew much of our history if any. I hadn't exactly been forthcoming about it even after things had gone down. "I thought you said you didn't want to date."

I sat back in my chair as they all looked at me expectantly. Jerome wasn't wrong in his assumption. While dating wasn't something I enjoyed, it's not like I hid my proclivities from my siblings. They probably knew about my dating life the same way I knew about theirs. Despite the fact that I wasn't celibate, I usually laid my desires out on the table clearly before fucking anybody. I didn't want to get anyone's hopes up that one or two nights might lead to more when I knew I had no desire to see them as anything more than a sexual partner.

Life wasn't a romance novel, and I was not going to suddenly develop feelings for any of them. I always made that abundantly clear from the jump.

"I'm not dating her," I answered honestly. "I asked her to marry me."

The silence that followed those words was loud. All eyes were on me as I calmly picked my fork back up and continued eating. I would let the information sink in, then let them ask their questions. I was surprised when none came. When I looked around, it was like sitting in a room full of statues. If not for the blinking, I'd have wondered if the world had frozen and I was the only one left with a full range of motion.

"Are you kidding me right now?" Jameson asked.

"When have you known me to joke about marriage?" I asked. "We haven't set a date just yet."

"What do you mean, you haven't set a date? You're going to tell us that you're getting married, just like that? And to someone who clearly only wants you for money or the company?" Jennifer's voice went shrill as she leaned over her plate. "Does this woman have something on you that's leading you to make this rash ass decision?"

I sighed. I'd known this probably wouldn't go over well, but I wasn't quite prepared to answer all their questions. Regina clearly was correct in thinking we needed to get together to discuss things so we could set the story straight. If people were already talking after just seeing us have dinner together, then I knew it was going to turn into a bigger deal once they found out we were engaged. I knew I could trust my siblings to keep their mouths shut, but no one else would be as discerning.

"No. I was the one who asked her to marry me. She only agreed a couple days ago."

Jalissa put a hand on my arm. "It's not that we don't think you can make good decisions. Clearly, we think you can since none of us wanted to fight for running the shit show that is the family company. We're just a little worried that maybe the stress is getting to you and you're having some early form of midlife crisis."

I could appreciate her words, and I knew it came from a place of thoughtfulness. Still, I was growing rather frustrated at the pushback. I may have been impulsive when asking Regina to marry me, but the more I thought about it, the more I knew and felt it was right. It was a strange thought that I had initially gone with emotion over taking the time to think everything out step by step. But I was finding as I retroactively considered things that the outcome would have been inevitable.

"This isn't a stress-induced action," I replied carefully. I didn't want them to think I wasn't taking their thoughts and feelings into account with my decision. However, I wasn't about to run the risk of losing Regina again just for the family. I'd lived my life for over thirty years for this family, and now it was time to do something for me. Something that I knew if I didn't try to grasp hold of before it slipped out of my fingers that I would regret. I didn't want to be an old man thinking back on my life and wishing I had taken that chance. Being in business meant taking risks, and while I had only done so in the context of work, I was now prepared to do so in my social life.

"Jameson knows who Regina is, and I'm sure the rest of you other than Jerome have heard of her before," I began. I knew they would continue to have reservations, but they also deserved to have some background information so they could make a better-informed decision on how they wanted to handle things. "Regina and I met as kids and at one point were in a relationship."

Jennifer nodded slowly. "Okay. So, what happened to your relationship? I haven't heard her name mentioned even once in the past few years."

"Father happened," I said. I wasn't about to mince words for him. "He didn't approve of the relationship, and back then, I was too weak-willed to fight for what I actually wanted."

I knew that was something all of us could understand. Some of us more than others.

"So, you what? Gave up on the relationship?"

I shook my head. "I did some hurtful shit, and she showed me the door. After, she ended up leaving the country, and we never spoke again until she came back a couple weeks ago."

"And now, somehow you guys are engaged," Jerome said, giving me a considering look. "How does that make any sense?"

"It doesn't need to."

Truthfully, I didn't know how to explain it in a way that would be a satisfactory answer. My brain agreed with them. The way I was going about this didn't make any logical sense. I could probably chalk it up to keeping your enemy close, but Regina wasn't influential enough to raise any call for alarm. Dummond Enterprises was powerful enough to weather most storms, and those who could potentially cause harm wouldn't risk it at this junction. Not according to the feelers I had out, anyway.

No. This decision I had rushed through was based on something else entirely, and I wasn't ready to cop to that verbally. I was still trying to reconcile it in my own mind.

Emotion. Being ruled by emotion wasn't something I was accustomed to when it came to anything other than anger. That, I was fully familiar with. But this...this feeling of want beyond all consequence was strange and new. I wasn't sure myself if it was going to work out or instead come back to bite me in the ass.

"Are you thinking with your heart or your dick?"

"Jesus, Jennifer!"

I looked over at her. She was looking back at me steadily in that way that always reminded me that if not for me taking the helm, she would have been the next best choice.

She was so much like our father, though I knew deep down she hated it. Still, her question was a fair one and got to the heart of things. Thinking with my dick was something our father would have understood, and while he might not have approved, he would have forgiven it in favor of youthful indiscretion.

"I mean, it's a fair question," Jameson said. He looked over at me expectantly. "I know how sideways things went with Regina, but you never really mentioned her after she left, so I'm not sure where this is all coming from."

Talking about this shit was not something I wanted to do, but it wouldn't be fair to tell them to deal with the decisions I made without questioning me. That was the way our father had done things, and I was actively trying not to be him. Still, it was attractive in a way it shouldn't be to think about doing what I wanted and telling them to just deal with it.

"Both." It wasn't a lie. It just wasn't as fifty-fifty as the word implied. My dick certainly liked the idea of Regina being bound to me even after years of absence. But it was the way just seeing her had my heart racing that had me taking notice. I never felt like that with anyone. It had something strange burning in my stomach, and I needed to understand it. I needed them to not give me grief about it while I worked through just what the fuck this meant. "I like her."

Jerome raised his eyebrows but didn't comment. Jalissa's considering look had me wanting to look away, but I held firm. I wouldn't back down with this. I had taken the easy route back then, and it led me into this mess in the first place.

"And does she like you?" Jennifer asked. "From what you've said, it sounds like things ended poorly between the two of you, so I'm surprised she would agree to even be around you. No, there has to be something more."

Jameson snorted. "Our father was involved, so of course, there's something more. She wants you to sign over a part of the business, which means he probably fucked over her entire family. I don't trust this shit, but if you like her—"

"I won't let my relationship affect you," I cut in. "I agreed to be the head of this family, and that comes first. But I am asking you, all of you, to trust me."

"We trust you, bro," Jerome spoke up. "One for all, all for the family and all that shit. Now, can we finish eating so I can go? I have plans."

I relaxed slightly when Jennifer and Jalissa started in on him, asking about his plans. I didn't doubt that he changed the subject for my benefit, and I made a note to thank him in some way later. As abrasive as Jerome could be, he hated conflict, especially when it came to his siblings. I gave him a lot of shit, but I was hopeful he was going to turn out better than the rest of us.

"You sure you want to do this?" I turned to look at Jameson. He had pitched his question just for the two of us, and I appreciated it. "I know the two of you had something back then, but people change, and not always for the better."

He wasn't wrong. By all previous accounts, our father hadn't started out his life being a bastard, but he certainly had ended things that way. Regina had changed in so many noticeable ways, yet there was something still there of the old her. The girl who had smiled at me and calmed me in ways I hadn't appreciated when I was fighting hard to fill shoes that were never meant for me. I had taken for granted having someone like her in my corner, but I wasn't giving that up now.

"Yes."

I had initiated this, and I would follow it to the end.

Chapter Ten

Regina

Today needed to be set on fire. I had dealt with not one but two contacts backing out of deals we had thoroughly rehashed weeks ago, and I was reaching my wit's end. Clearly, Liam and Elizabeth's reach extended further than I had originally thought, and now I was dealing with the fallout. I sighed as I sat back in my chair and stared out the window. I'd needed those two in order to secure the spaces I scouted for Mayfield Group's foray back into the restaurant business. In Atlanta, the location was just as important as the food you served and the ambiance provided. You could have the best food in the world, but if you were in a horrid location, shit would go south quickly.

But now, thanks to one minor overstep, I was having to decide whether or not to go back to the drawing board and scout out new locations or try to find a way to sweeten the deal with the limited funds available. Name dropping wasn't an option.

Or was it?

I had said yes to Jonathan but hadn't taken the whole thing seriously as of yet. The man was one pancake short of a stack, and his impulsivity was jarring. I was used to the calculating side of his family. If not for the fact it happened to my family, I could almost be impressed with his father's systematic dismantling of the community-based goodwill the Mayfields had gathered over the years in business. I would never know how long he had planned things, but the end result had been devastating.

Now, his son was offering himself up on a veritable platter. I didn't doubt Jonathan would do what he had to if I pushed things past a point, but that was also enticing. What would he do? Would he react like his dad, or would the barely-there control he had become famous for snap? I shivered at the thought of being on the other end of some unknown retribution at his hand. Maybe my friends back in London were right and I did have a death wish. At the thought of them, I checked the clock before grabbing my cell.

"Hello, honey bean. How are you?"

It was impossible not to smile at Alison's greeting. If anyone could be compared to a ray of fucking sunshine, it was her. I rarely remembered seeing a frown from her, which made it even more terrifying that she was the head of her family's luxury watch business.

We had met at a fashion event I hadn't even wanted to attend. She hadn't wanted to be there either, and both of our expressions showed the shared sentiment clearly. We had gotten to talking and quickly become friends. Besides Casey, Alison was my closest friend and the one I had divulged most of my plans to before I left.

"Oh, you know. Planning world domination and what I'm going to make for dinner. Same old."

Her giggle had me feeling lighter than before, and I knew calling her had been the best idea.

"You always did aim high. How are things with the hunky big bad?"

"Who?" I knew exactly who she was talking about but feigned confusion anyway while I thought how best to address the most recent changes.

"You know exactly who I mean," she pushed, calling me on my shit like always. "And don't even try to pretend you don't. Jonathan Dummond was all you talked about for months before you left. I don't believe for a second that you haven't already confronted him and dumped his body in a landfill somewhere."

"You are far more devious than people give you credit for."

"Thank you," Alison replied. "But back to business. I've seen pictures, and the man is fit. Please tell me you've seduced him with your feminine wiles. You two would make the cutest babies."

Jesus. She was going from zero to infinity way too fast. I might have wanted to climb the man like a tree, but kids were not even a thought in my mind, regardless of partner. Casey had that handled enough that I didn't need to worry about it.

"Anyway, details. All of them."

I tapped my pen on the desk as I thought about what to tell her. She wasn't far off with her thoughts of Jonathan, and I knew this latest news would have her running out and trying on bridesmaid dresses before the night was through.

"Fucked up and shot myself in the foot already when it came to a couple contacts. That was great." She made a considering noise but didn't say anything. "Found out my brother-in-law might be cheating but haven't talked to Casey since that confrontation. And Jonathan asked me to marry him. Just a pretty normal past two weeks."

The silence on the other end of the call would have been worrying if not for hearing Alison breathing over the line. I gave her time to gather her thoughts, given I had essentially smacked her in the face with a whole wall of fucked-up information. Hell, I was still recalibrating, and I was in it. Two weeks was feeling a lot like two years with as much as had happened. Half the time when I woke up, it still took me a few minutes to realize I wasn't in my bed in London but instead back in my home city. It was a jarring change.

Even more jarring was just how much like home Atlanta was starting to feel. I hadn't planned on staying past getting things set up and maybe taking a few trips back to visit the locations, but now I was starting to wonder how in the world I managed to stay away for so long.

"Alright. That was a lot to take in." I chuckled but didn't deny it. The whole situation was a lot to take in. "So, he wants you to marry him. He must have been carrying a torch for you this whole time."

That did get a reaction out of me, but not one I wanted to cop to. The idea that Jonathan carried a torch for anyone was laughable. The man was stone-faced on the best of days. No, I knew his type. This proposition was all business.

"Doubtful."

"Is he gay?"

"Not that I know of," I replied. "But these types of guys don't do relationships built on actual feelings. It's all about arrangements and appearances with them. Having me as a wife does nothing for his image."

"I don't know about that," Alison countered. "You're gorgeous as fuck with an Oxford education and a successful business. You have more to offer than like ninety percent of the planet."

Her confidence in me was sweet but still at odds to the market I now found myself in. Atlanta was much different than London. It wasn't just about your pedigree. Here you had to know exactly where to show up and how to show out to get noticed.

"Well, thank you kindly for the confidence boost. But I guarantee you, his proposal was only to keep me in line and in control. Besides, I don't need his help. I can get this business going on my own." I was adamant of that.

"You're not getting his help, though." She continued when I snorted. "You're not. Look at it this way. You're utilizing all the resources available to you like any smart business-minded person would."

I paused. That was certainly one way to look at things. Jonathan definitely had more far-reaching resources than I currently possessed. Could I leverage those for myself while also maintaining my independence? That might certainly make things worthwhile.

"Plus, you need to get laid, and he definitely looks good for that."

"Jesus, Alison!" I laughed. "Sometimes I wonder about you."

Her giggles brought another smile to my face. "So does my mother. Anyhow, I have got to get going, but think about what I said. Make this thing work for you."

I nodded, though she couldn't see me. "I will."

"And have a little fun with the man while you're at it. Nothing wrong with a little fun while you take over the world. Ta!"

She hung up the phone before I could respond, and I shook my head as I put the phone down on my desk. As much as I wanted to wave off her suggestions, the seed had been planted. The feeling of Jonathan against me had sat heavy in my mind for days, and now it had found a new outlet. Maybe she was right. I was good at compartmentalizing things, so why not make it work for me? It's not like I could go out and have sex as it was. If anyone got wind that I was finding pleasure elsewhere, I knew it would damage my reputation even more.

No, Jonathan was seemingly the answer to many of my problems. As much as it annoyed me, I picked the phone back up and dialed a number. My heartbeat jumped as I waited for the call to connect.

~*~*~

"I was surprised when you called me."

I looked over the rim of my glass, meeting dark brown eyes. Jonathan looked relaxed as he sat across the table from me. His black suit fell perfectly over broad shoulders, and once again, I cursed the fact that he was so attractive. It was annoying the way my gaze would be caught the moment he walked by. No one should be able to have everything, and it made me want to strip him of even more.

"I told you before, we need to talk about this and get our story straight." I set my glass back down, not averting my gaze from his. "I won't allow you to mess this up for me."

Jonathan nodded sharply before sitting back in his chair and looking me up and down. It should be illegal to have a gaze like that. I forced myself to sit still, though I wanted to squirm at his heavy look. I was familiar with it, but not from him. When his eyes met mine again, I was surprised there weren't zaps of electricity between us. This instant attraction was the best part of hell, and it made me recall Alison's words.

"Also," I continued, "we need to settle on the parameters of what we are and aren't willing to do to sell this thing as genuine."

"It is genuine."

I frowned at his words. No, this was business. This was penance. This wasn't anything close to being real. Before I could reply, the waitress came over and took our orders. Her departure didn't restart the conversation, and Jonathan and I sat in silence for the next few minutes.

I wasn't sure what else to say to start things off. I had given myself a pep talk on the way to the restaurant, and I knew what I wanted to ask for, but it was still nerve-wracking, given what was at stake. This could make or break my business here, and I had a lot more to lose if everything fell through.

"What are you hoping to get from our marriage?" Jonathan's question wasn't unexpected, and I appreciated him getting straight to the point.

I leaned forward, propping my chin against the back of my hands. Jonathan was quiet as he waited for me to speak, but I took my time choosing my words.

"This is a way for your family to help me rebuild the business your father destroyed. I need an in to get contracts signed and agreements in place, and that's where your reputation comes in." I paused for a moment, letting that sink in and gauging his reaction. I hadn't hidden my desire to use him for clout before, but it was different laying out my plan altogether.

"Have you been having difficulty securing—"

"I don't want to talk business with you," I said, cutting him off. That was one area where I had no desire for us to join. My business was my business, and I didn't need him butting in and messing things up for me or trying to take control.

Jonathan raised an eyebrow. "It'll be damn near impossible for me to provide you with assistance if I don't know what you plan on doing. If you're worried I'll jump in and tell you how to run things, you shouldn't be. That was not my intention. I have enough to deal at Dummond Enterprises."

I knew he had a point, but I still didn't want to give in to him. Something inside of me wanted the fight. I wanted to see just how far he would go with this. I didn't believe for a second that he wouldn't insert himself into my business, and I held no illusions he wouldn't happily take over if it suited him.

"You really expect me to trust you just like that?" I asked, giving him a pointed look. "I know you say you aren't aware of what your father did, but regardless, why do you think I should trust you? As far as I'm concerned, your decision-making has done nothing but make life more difficult for me."

"You have a point," he conceded. The conversation paused when our food was delivered, and I was happy to have something else to focus on.

The sounds around us slowly filtered in, and I marveled at just how easy it was for the rest of the world to melt away when I was talking to Jonathan. It was slightly worrying. I couldn't afford to be caught unawares. You never knew what ears were listening, just waiting for the chance to fuck things up for you. I had learned that the hard way, and I wasn't trying to deal with it again.

When Jonathan spoke again, I was surprised. "Perhaps we should draw up a contract. Outline the details so there won't be any confusion or contention when it comes to what is and isn't allowed between us."

As much as I wanted to deny it, he had a good point. It was something I had also been considering. I looked up at him from beneath my lashes before nodding. "We should."

"Good. I'll have my lawyer draw one up for your review." His confidence would have been sexy if not for my desire to hate him. "Unless you would like to have one drafted yourself?"

I waved my hand. "No. You are more than welcome to handle that. Email it to me once you're done, and I'll make sure you haven't put anything fucked-up into it."

"What kinds of fucked-up things do you think I would add?" he asked. He didn't look up from where he was cutting his steak, but I didn't mistake that for him being nonchalant. The hairs on the back of my neck stood up, and a new type of tension filled me. It was starting. When Jonathan glanced up, I saw a familiar glint in his eyes. It was similar to the one in my own gaze when I was planning something.

"I won't claim to know what depraved things your mind can conjure up," I replied, not rising to the bait. I could feel his eyes still on me as my fork sank into my chicken. I ate slowly and with care as if his gaze had no effect on me. In truth, it was heavy like a physical caress. How the hell did he turn it on like that? Never had I been so unnerved by someone's eyes being on me. "I'll have my lawyers review and get it back to you as soon as possible. I don't want to go too long without us being on the same page with this ruse."

"Is it a ruse?" he asked quietly. At my raised eyebrow, he shrugged. "I have nothing financially to gain from our union. For me, this is not about business but making amends."

That had me putting my fork down. "Making amends? You asked me to marry you to make amends?"

"I thought I made myself clear in that."

"Nothing with you is clear, Jonathan," I replied honestly. If not for wanting to get everything out, I would have regretted being so honest. Then again, why did it matter to me?

I was unbothered by Jonathan getting upset when he had clearly invited this into his life to begin with. I didn't ask to run into him, and I didn't ask for him to stick his nose into my business. But Alison was right. I would be doing myself a disservice by not utilizing all the resources available to me, and if Jonathan wanted to be a resource, I would use him until I had what I wanted.

For a moment, the only sounds between us were the clinking of utensils on our plates as we slowly ate our meal. I was in no hurry to return to my stale and lonely office. Sure, I had things I needed to do, but it was a far cry from the warmth of my father's office back in London where I was surrounded by family and others who wanted to see us succeed. Starting over was a lonely process, I was discovering. My dad had warned me of this, but I hadn't realized just how solitary it would be. I was the only person currently employed in this subsidiary, though I was confident once I could lock a few things down, that would change.

Jonathan sat his fork down before turning his attention back to me. "I apologize for being unclear in my intentions, but none of this is strictly business for me." When he looked back up at me, the expression in his eyes gave me pause. There was a rugged determination there. A sense of strength that explained why he was chosen to run an enterprise that employed thousands. I wanted to hold onto my anger, but I couldn't help but be impressed.

"Why?" It was a question that had been turning over in my mind for years. Why had this all happened? Why did I feel like it was my fault? Why did I feel the need to return?

Why was I still drawn to him?

"Because I want you."

Chapter Eleven

Jonathan

Around us, the world still moved as people came and left the dining area. But in the cocoon that had fallen, trapping us alone inside, there was only silence to follow my confession. A better man would have probably kept that close to his chest, giving some vague assurances of wanting to keep things strictly about righting the wrongs of a father driven by greed and the need to be in control. But I was not a better man. I was bitter.

The years had been long, and the desire for more damn near overwhelming as I realized what I did and didn't want in life. The company would stand, and I would remain at the helm as long as needed, but I refused to let my personal life fall aside for the desires of a dead man. Regardless of whether or not I would have realized this without Regina returning, the knowledge was here now, and fighting against it would only be denying myself what I wanted.

"Why the hell do you want me?"

"Why the hell wouldn't I?" My answer was partially a play on her response, but it was also the truth. How anyone could look at Regina, or better yet, get to know the fiery woman full of determination and not want her in their corner was strange to me. She had a stubborn streak to match my own, and I could only groan at the thought of that push and pull behind closed doors. Imagining it in the bedroom had me wishing we had met under better circumstances when I wasn't so full of adoration for a man only concerned with himself.

"Can I be frank?" Regina raised an eyebrow but gestured for me to go ahead. "I have few regrets in my life, but the one that does stand out is how I treated you. A better man would have realized what he had then, but I was not."

"But you realize that now?"

I nodded sharply. "I do."

"And this has nothing to do with the fact that Liam was courting me for his own bed and everything to do with you just realizing you…like me?"

I could lie and say yes. No one would know the truth of it but me, but honestly, I was tired of holding all the cards close to me and not revealing them until absolutely necessary. My father had done that, and now here I was, left to pick up the pieces of a family I didn't break. Did I really want to leave it to my siblings? To my future children?

I wanted to be better than my father, and that started with taking chances at being the opposite of him.

"Yes and no." When she leaned back and crossed her arms, I knew I was going to have an uphill battle on my hands. "You are right in thinking I didn't want you to do business with Liam. He and his father run a company that'll one day have them behind bars and hoping for parole. I didn't want you mixed up with that."

Regina didn't move, but I figured the fact she hadn't yet told me to fuck off was probably a win. I knew she didn't want nor need me hovering behind her like an overzealous parent, but I couldn't help but want to keep her from getting involved with the wrong people.

The Boldens might have enough money and connections to keep themselves from ever serving a day locked up, but I couldn't say the same for Regina.

"But I also do like you."

"Jonathan, you don't know me. Not anymore."

I nodded, acknowledging the truth in her words. "I might not fully know who you've become, but I know the woman you were, and I'm pretty sure she still exists in there. I know you care for your family more than yourself, something we both have in common."

She stared at me a moment before snorting softly. "Fine, so you know some things."

"Just a few," I agreed. "And I know you're attracted to me."

"You're a cocky son of a bitch."

I quirked my lips up. "Confident. But I'm even more attracted to you, so you have me by the balls again, I suppose."

Regina tilted her head to the side as she smirked. "You did seem to enjoy that. I wonder what people would think if they knew you were kinky on top of an asshole."

"You underestimate the depravity of most people in my tax bracket. Including me." I was more than happy to admit that little kernel of truth when it resulted in her soft laughter. "Besides, you were the one who told me people thought I was celibate." I wasn't sure why, but for some reason, her chuckles died down after my words.

Silence fell between us again as we finished eating and our plates were taken away. I could sense Regina needed some time to think, and I needed to do my own due diligence to make sure I could handle what would surely be a fraught next couple of weeks. I needed to plan how to introduce her as my fiancée in a way that wouldn't invite too much whispering behind the scenes on the heels of the Elizabeth situation.

I waved away the question of dessert and paid the check. It wouldn't do to seem too pushy, and I did need to get back to work. I still had fires set by Braselton to put out if I ever wanted to have a peaceful day in the office. Inflicting my resulting bad mood on others after dealing with him was unkind, and my knuckles could only handle the punching bag for so many days in a row.

"Perhaps we should schedule dinner in a couple days to regroup and discuss things," I said as we stood to leave. I offered Regina my hand and waited patiently as she stared at it. This was the moment. We were in full view of anyone watching. If she rejected me, I had no doubt by the end of the day that one of my siblings would have heard about it. The breath I was holding left me lightheaded, but I blew it out silently when her smaller hand gracefully answered mine.

"That sounds like a perfect idea." Regina looked up at me as I helped her from her seat. What I wouldn't give for this to be an entirely different situation where I could pull her in and touch that warmth. If I had my arms around her, I knew letting her go would be impossible of a feat. As it was, just having her hand in mine had me ravenous, craving to push harder and go farther. I wanted to surround her as completely as she had surrounded me so long ago. How I ever thought I had gotten over her was a mystery now that these feelings had been unearthed. I had been a fool to let her go, but I wasn't the same boy I was.

I guaranteed myself I would show her that, no matter what it took.

~*~*~

I grit my teeth as I stared at the computer screen. Two days had turned into three, and with each hour that passed since I'd sent Regina the contract for her to review, I found myself growing worried something may have triggered her anger. The contract had been simple enough, akin to the prenuptial agreement I had on hand from the one or two disastrous times I had almost let father convince me that marrying someone of his choosing was a better idea than risking my own relationship skills or lack thereof.

While I had never been celibate since I learned my dick was for more than pissing, actual relationships with no ulterior motives beyond enjoying one another's company were few and far between. To my knowledge, only two of my siblings had a regular thing going, and only one was public.

A knock on my office door caught my attention, and I called out, telling the person to come in. When the door opened, I was surprised to see Kevin. I had seen him again once or twice, mostly when I was looking for Curtis for updates. He hadn't sought me out on his own, so his presence now was enough to make me pause.

"Kevin."

"I apologize for barging in, sir. But I had some information that..." He trailed off for a moment before seeming to gather what little courage he possessed and standing straighter. "Curtis had informed me you wanted an audit of a few of the smaller subsidiaries, and he assigned them to me."

I nodded and waved him in, telling him to close the door behind himself. I didn't need anyone walking by to overhear our conversation. The few searches I'd wanted done were on some entities I had previously been unaware of and ones father had never mentioned. It wasn't uncommon for him to neglect certain areas, but these seemed especially singled out.

Kevin handed me a thick folder before taking a seat across from me. "This is a large amount of information," I said glancing up at him.

He nodded quickly. "It is. I wrote summaries of each subsidiary including establishment date, rationale, and the fields they cover. I included financials, though there were some missing pieces that...well, you can see for yourself, I'm sure. All the documents are there in their original forms."

I raised an eyebrow before looking back down at the folder. Taking a moment to compose myself, I set it on my desk before leaning back in my seat and crossing my arms. "There are some things in there that have you worried, aren't there?"

Kevin folded his hands together before unclasping them again. It was clear he was nervous, but I wasn't in the right headspace to seem more friendly. Besides, if he was going to follow Curtis, he was going to have to get over his nerves at me being less than friendly. I didn't have time for it.

"Well, sir—"

"You can call me Jonathan," I interrupted. "If I'm going to rely on you, we should be on a first-name basis."

He nodded again. "Right, of course, sir. Jonathan." I blinked slowly as he took a deep breath in. "Most of what I found was expected. There was some fudging of numbers that would need to be double-checked, but the biggest issue was with Patterson Construction."

I frowned. That name sounded familiar, but it was common enough that I could be thinking of something else. "What were they involved in?" I asked before opening the folder. The papers were organized much the same way I kept my own documents, which I could appreciate. It gave me hope that when Curtis did put in for retirement, the division wouldn't fall apart.

"They supposedly built a few of the warehouses as well as a luxury residential subdivision down in Glasgow near the Florida border."

His wording caught my attention, and I looked up at him. "Supposedly?" I narrowed my eyes when he nodded. "Explain."

"Well," Kevin began. He folded his hands again, and I fought the urge to tell him to sit still. Being a dick wouldn't help the situation, so I wisely stayed quiet and waited for him to continue. "I remembered we had run an audit on properties six months ago, and I didn't remember seeing anything luxury in that part of the state. Most of the properties are centered around the metro Atlanta area and Savannah."

I nodded in agreement. Real estate had been father's pet project, and he had always had a strong distaste for rural areas. I didn't get it, but my own portfolio was similarly concentrated, so I had never said something in favor of not appearing hypocritical.

"So, it was missed in the previous audit?"

Kevin shook his head. "No. I mean, I suppose. But the biggest issue was when I looked into the address of the property itself." He gestured at another group of papers, and I picked them up. My eyebrows shot up when I read over his findings, and I looked at him sharply.

"Is this correct? Definitively?"

His shoulders jerked like he was about to shrug before he cleared his throat and nodded slowly. "The property doesn't exist. The land is there, but there's nothing but a field and a mailbox."

I clenched my jaw and glared back down at the paperwork. The picture was just as Kevin said, and I could see by the timestamps that it was taken roughly four months ago. That didn't explain why the property was said to have been completed twenty years ago. Something wasn't adding up, but I damn sure planned to get to the bottom of it.

Chapter Twelve

Regina

I stared at the front door of Casey's townhome wondering what would greet me once I went in. The past two weeks had been silent with little more than an errant text sent here and there, letting me know she was alive but needed space. I had happily given it to her and carried on with my own business, but enough was enough. Now not only did I have to worry about her being upset with me when it came to Ray, I also had my own fucked-up shit to inform her of, and I wasn't sure which would be the worst to her.

Liam had called me once or twice since he had last left me that message. I never answered. As far as I was concerned, his usefulness had expired, so I was no longer interested in entertaining him. How he could still think I would answer his calls, I had no idea. Then again, ego was a hell of a drug, and he was no doubt an addict. Christa had mentioned him the couple times we got lunch or dinner together, but even she didn't seem as pushy about me seeing him as I thought she would be. Especially not with me casually dropping that Jonathan and I had been seeing one another. I hadn't clarified in what way yet, but once he and I met tomorrow night, we would go public with it, and besides Casey, Christa was the first person I planned to inform. If she heard that bit of news from anyone else, I knew she would take it personally, and I needed every bit of goodwill from her that I could cultivate.

The contract Jonathan's lawyer had sent over was fairly simplistic. Still, I had my lawyer pick through it like a fine-toothed comb, looking for anything that might come back unfavorably against me. The biggest surprise to me had been the length of his terms. A one-year engagement and four years of marriage, after which I could divorce him and walk away with enough money to buy a city block and then some. I couldn't help but wonder if these same terms had been provided to the other women who'd graced his orbit.

"Of course, they were," I grumbled to myself. "No point in thinking I'm special."

The thought of it made something hot and ugly well up within me. I pushed the feeling down and thought about the future. I couldn't afford to get off target. I needed to get a foothold into this dining market, and I had to be aggressive. I looked back up at Casey's townhome. But first I needed to talk to my sister before I got lost in my own head. I still didn't want to involve her in the business side of things, but I needed to talk to someone about this thing with Jonathan before I got locked up for talking to myself.

I also needed someone to help me figure out what exactly he did know. It was hard for me to believe that Jonathan was truly in the dark about his father's shit behavior over the years. He spoke like he was also pissed off at things, but that's what these guys did. They played games. I should know; I was attempting to do the same. And yet, my intuition told me his words had rang true. Intuition had gotten me through some shit times over the years, and so when she made an appearance, I usually made a point to listen. I hadn't when it came to Liam and now look where it had gotten me.

My cell ringing startled me, and I connected the call on my steering wheel. "Hello?"

"Are you planning on coming in or sitting in the driveway all day?"

I looked up to see Casey standing in the now open doorway with her hands on her hips. With a nod, I disconnected the call and climbed out of the car. Once I got closer, I could see her face better. Her eyes were still slightly puffy, no doubt from crying one too many tears, and her face was bare of makeup. Her thick hair was pulled into a high bun, and the few curls poking out looked fuzzy and dry.

"You look like shit." Her huff of laughter held little amusement, but she fell easily enough into my hug. I wrapped my arms around her. "Can I kill him yet?"

Casey pulled back with a small smile and shook her head. "Not yet. He wants to talk to you, though, if that's okay."

I sneered but let myself be pulled into the house. The only talking I wanted to do was with my fists or maybe the heel of my shoe, but still, I would follow Casey's lead. She was the one in charge here. I knew it, and Ray damn well better know it too.

The house was eerily quiet as we walked into the living room, and I asked where the boys were so I could figure out if I needed to adjust the language on the tip of my tongue.

"They're at Ray's parents' place for the next couple days while Ray and I...talk," Casey replied as we walked through the doorway of the living room. The room was still brighter than it had any right to be after everything that had happened.

It was too cheerful. Too much like nothing bad had even occurred, and I hated it. I wanted the world to be dark and gray to match my mood.

Ray was standing near the window staring at the back yard. The few times I had seen him, he was always in a suit, but now he was dressed down in rumpled-looking sweats. He wasn't looking casket sharp, but you didn't need to look good to be cremated. When he turned to look at us walking in, I smiled sharply, delighting in the fact that he also looked like he'd been hit with a 'fuck you' stick.

"Ray," I said coolly. He nodded at me before walking around the couch. I raised an eyebrow, and he wisely got the hint and kept the coffee table between us before sitting on the far side of the couch.Casey sat beside him, not close enough to be touching but still too fucking close in my opinion. I sat in the single chair, not trusting myself to even be on the same piece of furniture as him. Being in the same house was enough as is.

"Hey, Regina," he replied. "Thanks for coming."

"Casey asked me to, so I came." I narrowed my eyes. "I'm not doing this for you. Let me make that clear from the jump."

He swallowed before nodding again and looking down at his hands. "Right. Well, regardless, thank you. This hasn't been easy, and I wanted to clear up—"

"Are you seriously about to tell me it wasn't what it looked like?" I asked him, raising my voice slightly.

Casey held up a hand. "Please, Regina. Let him explain." She looked at me beseechingly, and I huffed out a breath before sitting back and crossing my arms. Ray glanced at Casey before looking back at me.

"I know you don't want me to say it, but it wasn't what it looked like. It was all business with me and Elizabeth." When I scoffed, he stood up. "See, I told you she wouldn't listen."

Casey sighed, and I almost felt bad about stressing her out until I remembered what I saw. Sure, Ray and Elizabeth hadn't been fucking on the table, but the whole situation looked far too intimate for a simple business dinner. And the fact that he hadn't told Casey was another strike against him.

"Regina, just give him a chance."

"Fine," I bit out. I glared up at Ray. "Explain to me like I'm fucking five then, brother. You were just brushing something off her hand, right? Were you trying to fuck some business into your portfolio?"

Ray's eyes narrowed. "What? Like you?"

I frowned. "The fuck are you talking about?"

His smile wasn't the least bit humorous as he walked back over to the couch.

"You think I haven't heard about you and Jonathan? Or how you two were caught coming out of an office together twice? You're one to talk when you haven't even told Casey about that."

Casey whipped her head back around and stared at me, surprise etched onto her face. "What? You were with Jonathan?"

I ground my teeth before answering, "Yes. He was at the restaurant when I first went to meet Christa, and we've met for meals a couple times."

"The same Jonathan Dummond whose family royally fucked yours and bankrupted your parents' business," Ray added, no doubt gloating that the attention was now off him and his cheating ass. "The same family that got your sister's scholarship cancelled, but I'm sure you don't know anything about that. Right?"

"What?" I looked over at Casey, who was now looking down. "What is he talking about, Casey?"

She sighed before leaning back against the couch. "My scholarship to Georgia Tech was cancelled a couple months after you left. I was never given a satisfactory answer, but a couple weeks later, an application to the Dummond Enterprises scholarship fund came in the mail, and I knew."

"That motherfucker!" I shouted. Energy coursed through me, and I stood up, needing to move to keep from slamming something. I paced for a moment before turning back to Casey. "Why did you never tell me this before? How did you finish without—"

"How the fuck do you think?" Ray cut in. "My family paid for it."

"As what? A fucking dowry?" I was seething. Hot, pulsing anger rushed through my veins. "So now what? You own Casey? You can cheat on her whenever you like? Over my fucking dead body, and by mine, I mean yours."

Casey stood up as I walked toward him and came at me with her hands out. "No! Regina, no."

"I wasn't cheating on her!" Ray's shout echoed through the room, but I only stopped when Casey's hands gripped my arms, halting my motions. "It wasn't my idea to have dinner with Elizabeth, but I needed her to get shit on Liam."

Liam's name had me freezing. How had this conversation led back to him? "What? Why do you need shit on Liam?"

Ray scrubbed a hand over his face before sitting back down on the sofa. "Because there's apparently someone on his payroll fucking things up at my uncle's company, and it has his name all over it." When he looked up at me, his face looked tired in a way I understood. It was the same look I'd seen on my dad's face for weeks after we had left. "Elizabeth had been willing to meet with me and give me some leads, though she refused to help any more than that. And now, she's gone silent after the shit at the restaurant."

I stared at him as I considered his words. Now knowing the type of business Liam was involved in, it didn't surprise me he might have someone feeding him intel on the competition. Hell, I would be surprised if Jonathan wasn't engaged in the same thing.

"Why didn't you just tell Casey what was going on, then?" I countered. "Why be vague and leave it open for misinterpretation at all?"

Ray shrugged. "I didn't think it was important to talk about. I've always done my best to keep Casey out of anything business-related because of what happened with you guys. Plus, Elizabeth and I were only going to meet once and that was it."

I took in his explanation for a moment before turning to Casey. "What do you think about all this?"

She sighed. "While I don't appreciate Ray keeping me in the dark about things like this," she began, "I do understand why he didn't tell me. I don't like hearing about these bullshit cat and mouse games you all seem to be involved in."

I sat back down in the chair and fought the urge to scrub a hand over my own face. Things had just gotten complicated in a completely different way. I could admit that Ray's story seemed plausible, though I didn't like it. Our worlds were too fucking close for comfort, and I knew I needed to come clean about some things to make sure there were no other issues.

"Liam was one of the people who reached out to me about doing business with him," I said. Casey frowned, but

Ray's expression was surprised. "He had some connections in real estate I needed to utilize, particularly when it came to permits. But after the shit with Elizabeth, he came back saying he could no longer work with me, and as you can guess, those connections dried up."

"Damn it," Ray bit out. "He's got his hands in everything, but I feel like there's someone else pulling the damn strings. He's poached some of our best engineers and two development projects that cost us millions. If we could figure out how he's getting the information…"

When he trailed off and looked at me beseechingly, I almost felt bad squashing that tiny bit of hope. I doubted Liam would rethink business with me, and even if he did, the cost of rekindling that relationship might be more than I could give.

"I can't make any promises," I said carefully. "But I'll talk to Jonathan and see if he's heard anything."

"And why would Jonathan tell you anything?"

I sucked my teeth as I thought about how much to tell them. No doubt everything would be front page news in a few days, so I should probably get ahead of it now with Casey. But the revelation that Jonathan's dad had somehow fucked her over too had me gnashing my teeth together.

"Because…we're engaged."

Chapter Thirteen

Jonathan

I hadn't expected a message from Regina so quickly, but I couldn't deny it pleased me to have her response. There had been a small part of me that wondered if I needed to be more persistent in getting her to agree to this relationship, contracted or not. That part had fought against the knowledge that I knew she didn't like to be cornered. As thrilling as it would be to see just how far she might be willing to go against another person, I wasn't trying to have her fight me.

As it was, I was uncharacteristically nervous enough as I waited for her to show up at my front door. Having her in my own space was enough to leave me with too much time and not enough to do with it. The cleaning service I paid for was worth every penny, and I wouldn't know where to find the broom to begin with. Food had been made and was waiting on the table for us to be seated. Having something to do between us seemed to be the best way to keep our conversation flowing. As much as I would like the entirety of Regina's attention on me, I was still catching up to my own impulsivity and the resulting fallout. All of this was new to me, and as much as I wanted it, I was wary.

My actions thus far had been so far out of the realm of my norm. Usually, I left the impulsive decisions to Jerome or Jameson. They were far better at deciding their moves without much thought and having things work out. The few times I tried to emulate them in my youth hadn't worked out well for me. No, I was much better at the long game—taking my time to think through each move and the resulting consequence before making my play. But the long game wouldn't work here. Regina was making plays faster than I was used to, so I needed to match her blow for blow to keep up.

The doorbell rang, jolting me from the pacing motions I had stumbled into, and I made my way to the door. When I opened it, I had to suck in a quick breath. Regina looked good in anything, but there was something about her in form-fitting fabrics that had me fighting back the need to touch.

"We have a problem," she said, breaking my perusal of her body. She walked by me, not bothering to wait for me to show her into the house, but instead of being annoyed, I was charmed. I knew my reputation with most people, even those in my tax bracket. None of them had ever been so bold with me, and I liked it that way. I would keep up appearances and show up when needed, but I had no desire to be friends.

But Regina was different. Sure, she was trying to play the game, a game most of us had been born into, yet she didn't seem to have the same almost malicious feel that others did. I knew she would bulldoze her way through people if needed, but it didn't seem she did it just for fun, more out of necessity.

"Well, come on in," I replied with a smirk. Regina glanced at me over her shoulder before rolling her eyes. I closed the door behind me and followed her into the living room. If it were anyone else, I would've had them out the door as fast as they had come in, but the hind part of my brain wanted Regina's scent on everything. If I had my way, she would never leave. "Dinner is ready if you're hungry."

She walked to the dining table and lifted up one of the plate covers. "Did you cook this?"

"I'm not trying to kill you," I replied, enjoying her soft chuckle. Like a gentleman, I pulled the chair out for her, guiding her to sit. "I hire out most of the household affairs, though you are more than welcome to suggest any changes you'd like."

"Why would I do that?" she asked as she placed the tray to the side.

"Are you not moving in?" I sat across from her and removed my own plate cover. "It'll be difficult to sell our engagement with us not physically living together."

Regina gave me a look. "I don't need to live with you to be with you. I don't remember seeing that anywhere in the contract, otherwise I would've had my lawyer strike it and called you up to give you some choice words."

I sighed and took a sip of the wine in front of me. "Regina, be reasonable. While I don't normally have guests over, there are people in this building who would notice if I routinely came and went without you on my arm."

"The people in your building need to mind their business then, clearly."

I snorted softly, but I didn't disagree with her on that. It was aggravating on a good day when something as innocuous as me ordering in a pizza two days in a row resulted in my mother calling to check if I was eating well. It was why I was so careful with the women I did choose to be with. Rarely did any of them make it to my residence. I had enough properties to make it work.

"You're probably right, but that doesn't change the fact that we need to be seen together regularly," I replied. "I didn't realize I needed to make the contract that specific, but we can amend as needed."

Regina sighed before picking up her own wine glass. She took a healthy sip before looking at me from under dark lashes. "Fine. I'll make myself seen here a few times a week." Her lips quirked up in a smirk. "If you wanted me in your space that badly, all you had to do is ask."

"If I had asked up front, you would have slapped me."

"Perhaps," she conceded. "Maybe I'm saving myself for marriage."

"Maybe you're full of shit," I cut back with a sharp smile. "It didn't seem like you were saving yourself when you had your hands around my neck and balls."

She shrugged, not looking the least bit repentant. "You were in my way. That reminds me." Her expression grew serious. "Did you know your father nearly fucked up my sister's chance at college?"

What the actual fuck? I had figured if I ever got a chance to speak with Regina again that we would have issues to hash out, but each new layer was peeled back to reveal another fucked-up layer in this cake of foolishness. And each time something new was revealed, I wanted to march down to the cemetery, dig my father up, and burn him. He wouldn't feel it, but it would make me feel better about the shit he left for me to clean up.

"How the fuck did he do that?" I couldn't help the growl in my voice. It seemed with each step forward I took, I was forced five steps back, and frankly, I was done with it.

I had hoped to take the slow and steady route of turning things around, but maybe I was playing it too damn safe. Maybe it was time to press harder. "No. How he did it doesn't matter. I apologize on his behalf."

Regina looked at me for a moment before setting her glass down. "You know what? At first, I thought you must be lying when you said you had no idea the things your dad had done. But now, I'm not so sure."

I wasn't sure what to make of that. It wasn't surprising that she hadn't trusted me at face value. Hell, I wouldn't have trusted myself either if I had been in her shoes. My father had thoroughly poisoned the well when it came to getting any leeway from Regina. It just made things more frustrating when I wanted to get her on my side. I needed some time to think without losing what little goodwill I had managed to garner from her. If this were anyone else, I would say I knew exactly how to do that. With Regina, the rules of engagement were so much more difficult to manage.

"Penny for your thoughts." I looked back up at her. Regina wasn't smiling, but amusement was clear in her gaze. "You looked to be deep in thought, and despite my better judgment, I'm curious."

"I think it's time for us to get serious about this," I said before leading us to the couch. This was a conversation that needed to happen, and now was the time to do it. "What are you looking to get from this?"

Regina raised an eyebrow. "Shouldn't I be the one asking you that? You were the one who proposed marriage for whatever reason."

"And you said yes," I pointed out. "I doubt I'm the first man to propose to you in your lifetime, yet from everything I could find, you haven't married."

"It's true you aren't the first man…or woman." She smirked when I gave her a considering look. "I always wondered if that was why you asked me to play mistress. So you could have a unicorn to fuck around with when things got stale. Hell, after the way your dad acted when he caught Jameson, I thought for sure he hated me because I dabbled myself."

I frowned as I let that information sink in. I was unconcerned about Regina's sexuality. It didn't matter to me as long as I was the one partnered with her. The implication that I might have brought her to bed with whoever I would've married had I not grown a backbone was one I didn't want to look too closely at. I couldn't totally rule it out.

"No," I said finally. "I had no idea you liked women, so I doubt my father did. He was caught by complete surprise with Jameson."

"And Jalissa?" Regina asked. At my surprised expression, she rolled her eyes. "You aren't the only one who does research."

I nodded. "As far as I know, he never figured it out. I don't know if she ever planned on telling him. He's dead now, so it doesn't matter regardless."

Regina sighed and leaned back against the couch, and my gaze followed, drawn like a moth to her flame. With her hair back in a bun, I got an unfettered view of the tempting skin around her neck and a hint of the perfume she wore. Everything in me wanted to fall into her and take that fragrance into myself until it soaked into my DNA.

"You're staring," she said.

"You're gorgeous." It was the truth, and not one I felt the need to hide. Watching her was quickly becoming my favorite pastime. "I want to kiss you."

That had her looking at me fully. "Are you drunk already?"

"I could say something foolish like I'm drunk on you, but you might take a swing at me."

"Possibly," she confirmed. Still, her gaze changed, and I could almost feel the air between us growing heated. I hadn't put anything in the contract about physical contact, but fuck had I wanted to.

"Let me kiss you."

"You have a funny way of asking."

I paused for a moment, but considering she hadn't left or reacted violently, I decided to take my chances. Before the silence could stretch, I reached out, cupping her cheek, and tried not to be distracted by how soft her skin was. It had only been a few months since the last time I was with someone, but I swore I had never felt something so decadent. Gravity drew me in until everything in my vision was her. When our lips met, the feeling was indescribable.

Falling into her was so fucking easy. Moving away wasn't an option, and so I leaned in further, our mouths pressing hungrily against one another. With a groan, I parted my lips, enjoying when she took the initiative, tongue darting forward without hesitation. When her hands reached up to grip my shoulders, another thrill ran through me. This passion was what I was missing. The push and pull between us was the best and worst type of foreplay, and finally, I felt I could breathe a sigh of relief. When Regina's teeth pressed down on my bottom lip, I couldn't stop myself from groaning, and when she pushed me back against the couch before climbing into my lap, I knew there was no coming back from this.

Chapter Fourteen

Regina

This was out of pocket even for me. I knew I should be keeping my distance and only treating this like the contracted relationship it was, yet I couldn't stop myself from darting my tongue into the heat of Jonathan's mouth. The taste of wine enhanced the flavor that was all him, and I wanted to glut myself on it.

The soft scratch of his chin against mine made me shiver, and I covered the reaction by pressing harder against him. This wasn't going to be some slow tango of love. This was to scratch an itch, a need that would be taken care of, and then we would move on. If I couldn't get it from anyone else without causing a scandal, then I would get it here, and I refused to think more about it.

"Maybe we should move this to the bedroom," Jonathan said, voice rumbling deeply like the threat of a storm. His hands felt large and hot against my hips, and I could feel him shifting a hard rod against my inner thigh. "Unless you want to stop."

We probably should. It would have been the smart thing to tell him this was a mistake and couldn't happen again. But when I found myself standing and pulling him up with me, I couldn't find it in me to regret it. I wanted him right now, and I didn't want to think about it. Nothing I had planned was going my way, and damn it, I just wanted to stop worrying about it if only for a little while.

When we walked into Jonathan's room, I quickly turned, pulling his head back down toward mine. I kept my kisses fast and hard, biting my anger at everything into the soft curve of his lip. I gripped the back of his neck while allowing him to walk me backwards until we both fell slowly onto the bed. The softness of it against me was so strangely at odds with the hard length of him against my front as he pressed me back. It was an intoxicating feeling and one I needed more of.

Clothes were peeled away until there was nothing between us but time and hurt being smothered by our moans as we continued feeding from one another. I could feel the hard length of Jonathan's cock sandwiched between us, and I shifted to get my hand around it.

"Fuck," Jonathan groaned before turning his head to press his lips against the skin of my neck. I let him, lifting my head to give him more space as kisses rained down against my throat. I bit my lip as I squeezed the length of him.

He wasn't the longest I had ever been with, but the hefty girth in my hand had me parting my legs to let him fall between them. I needed that thickness pressing into me until I forgot my name.

"Please tell me you have condoms somewhere within reach," I said before swallowing hard. My voice was rough as if I'd spent the afternoon smoking instead of worrying about all the shit I hadn't gotten done. "If you have to leave this bed before I'm done with you…"

Jonathan shook softly as he chuckled. I forced myself to still when the heat of his breath wafted over my skin, lighting me up. I gripped the back of his neck hard, but he shook off my hold before pushing up on his hands. His eyes were crinkled up in an expression I wasn't ready to make sense of.

"You'll have to let go of me so I can get to my drawer," he said, glancing down at where I still had my hand wrapped around him.

I pursed my lips before reluctantly letting go. "Fine. Hurry."

He raised an eyebrow. "You want me that bad?"

"Don't get cocky, asshole. It was either you or Liam, though if you make me wait any longer, I might reconsider." I was triumphant when his lips curled up in clear jealousy and his movements went jerky. I couldn't help but needle at him, and I reached my hands up, letting them rest above my head.

I knew what I looked like, and I smirked when his eyes moved back to me. The position had me arching my back, pushing my breasts up within easy reach. I didn't bother closing my legs, instead letting him see the slick between my thighs. There was no point in hiding how turned on I was. I was lying naked in his bed. Hiding was the last thing I planned on doing.

Jonathan stared, dark eyes full of heat as they roamed over my body. He sat back on his knees between my open thighs. His cock stood proudly, jerking slightly as his gaze centered on my pussy. I shifted my hips up and watched him suck in a sharp breath.

"Are you going to put that on or just stare at me?"

He glanced up with a smirk. "Both." I rolled my eyes but kept my gaze on him as he opened the packet and rolled the condom over his dick. My mouth went dry as one of his hands pressed against my inner thigh and he shifted. Time seemed to stop as he moved closer.

When the first push came, I sucked in a harsh breath. Everything was liquid heat, and I let my head fall back as

Jonathan's dick slid deep inside me. I heard his breath hitch, and I couldn't help but smirk at that little sound. He sank in, carving a space within me that had been begging to be filled for weeks. The hands curling tightly around my hips had me clenching down, and I knew I'd be feeling that touch even after I lay alone in my bed. But for now, in this fucked-up game of what my life had become, I had him.

The pace was slow and steady but dirty as fuck as Jonathan pulled back before thrusting again with a little twist. One hand curled under my knee, pressing up and opening my hips wider. I felt him thrust that much deeper, lighting up nerves that had me groaning into his neck. Sweat, salty yet somehow sweet, beaded his neck, and I licked, tasting him.

"Fuck, baby."

"Don't call me that, asshole," I hissed out before I sank my teeth into him. I felt more than heard his groan as it rumbled across my sensitive skin. The bastard was like a live wire, lighting me up each time his hips met mine. I wanted to fight against the moans that threatened to pour from my own lips, but one well-placed thrust had me abandoning that plan as I tossed my head back. "Oh fuck. Why the fuck is your dick so good?"

Jonathan's chuckle was low and sounded strained. Lips encircled my left nipple, and when it was taken between his teeth, another cry ripped itself from my throat. My nipples had always been sensitive, a fact he clearly remembered as I looked down and our eyes met.

Heat was too weak a word to describe the fire in his dark gaze. I felt consumed, cocooned in a wall of fire as my nerves sang out with pleasure. My hand snapped out, grabbing the back of his neck as he released my now-swollen nub.

"More." Pleasure made my voice gritty, and I pushed into his thrusts, wanting to tattoo each burst of pleasure into my very core. This was fucking. The type of fucking I had craved but thought I wouldn't have from this bunch of self-satisfied pricks. That it was Jonathan giving it to me should have been a surprise.

Then again, I had rarely been unsatisfied by our inexperienced forays into sex when we were younger. His learning curve had me thankful to his practice partners and furious that they dared have him like this. This possessiveness was new to me. I had never cared with previous partners, yet now, I could feel that green-eyed demon pushing me to grip tighter and kiss harder so he knew who the fuck he belonged to.

Mine.

We had a contract, and no matter how it started, it was binding. Until I was satisfied, this was all fucking mine.

"You taste so fucking good," Jonathan groaned, yanking my attention back to the present even as I clenched down on the cock that had me seeing stars. His mouth was shiny with spit, and I could see a similar sheen on my nipples. "Makes me want to taste you everywhere."

"So do it," I gasped out, pushing his head down. "You're always talking so much shit. Fucking do it."

Jonathan paused, his hips slowly withdrawing. I wanted to groan and yank him back against me. Damn my mouth. It had a habit of getting away from me. I was about to pull him back, but before I could, he shifted, lifting my legs up until they fell across his shoulders.

"Always so pushy."

I was going to tell him to fuck off, but my breath was caught at the first brush of his tongue against the lips of my cunt. I thought I was already heated, but it was nothing compared to the fire of feeling that came when that same wicked appendage pushed its way between my folds and sank deep into the core of me. Not pressing into the feeling was impossible, and I gave in to the addiction of having him exactly where I needed him—between my legs, making me come.

"Fuck," I hissed as I pressed my hips into him, enjoying the vibration from his moan and the tightening of his fingers on my thighs. I was held tight, trapped in my own pleasure as his mouth proceeded to carve out a place for him between my legs. "Yes."

How he knew every point to touch inside me, I didn't know. One of my hands gripped the sheets below me as I slid down further while the other cupped the back of his head to keep him from stopping. I could feel the cord holding back my orgasm threatening to snap, and I wanted it so badly I could taste it. When I finally fell, it was like being flung over a cliff, and I jerked up from the bed as I shouted. It had been so long since I last felt this, and a part of me was dismayed it was Jonathan sparking such feelings in me.

"You taste so goddamn good," he groaned when he could pull away. I said nothing as aftershocks shot through me, giving Jonathan time to crawl back up my body until our faces were even. He hesitated, but I didn't give a shit, pulling him down to me and covering his slick lips with mine.

The taste of myself had me shivering, and I pressed forward, seeking my own flavor in his mouth. "I'm not done with this yet," I said, wrapping my hand back around his dick. The condom was slippery with my own fluids, and I angled him back toward me. "Unless you need a break."

Jonathan chuckled before shifting to press forward again. It was only a moment before he was buried back deep inside, just where I needed him. I closed my eyes and let my head fall back. Lips brushed against my neck as they trailed up toward my ear.

"I'll never be done with you."

Shivers raced up and down my spine, but I didn't reply to his heated words. Threat or promise, it didn't matter. Tonight, I would let myself fall into him and forget everything left to come.

Chapter Fifteen

Jonathan

I groaned as I opened my eyes against the slant of sun that fell over my face. My body ached as if I had been worked hard at the gym, but I knew it was just from following Regina's lead until we both fell against one another in exhaustion. The length of her was still pressed tightly against me, and I couldn't find it in myself to regret anything. Long had I thought about having Regina in my bed, and the reality had been over and beyond anything my fantasies had cooked up. Fuck, just the memory of the hot squeeze of her pussy had my dick trying to rise up for another round.

Normally, I didn't linger in bed any longer than it took me to answer a few emails and talk myself out of fucking off to an island somewhere to not deal with people. Now, I found myself not wanting to leave. The scent of Regina was around me, soaking into my sheets. Was it strange to want to wrap yourself around someone until you forgot where you ended and they began? Was this how Jameson felt? If so, his bizarre behavior for the past few months made complete sense.

"I should probably apologize to him," I grunted to myself.

"You should not be thinking about some other man when you have your arms wrapped around me." I looked down to see Regina's eyes barely open but clearly on me. Her hair was stuck to one side of her head and there was a crease on her cheek from the pillow, yet she looked as beautiful as she had when she first walked in my door last night.

"I was talking about Jameson."

"Even worse." I snorted but watched closely as she stretched. I lifted my arms but didn't withdraw them. I wasn't ready for the space between us to grow again. "What time is it? Shouldn't you be at work?"

I shrugged, not feeling the least bit of urgency. "I don't know, but probably. You?"

Regina chuckled. "I'm a one-woman show. I get in when I get in." I was surprised when she didn't seem to be in a rush to pull away from me. "Are you going to move?"

"Hadn't planned on it," I answered honestly before taking a chance and placing my hand on her back. "Do you want me to move?"

"I mean, technically this is your bed," she said before settling back against the pillow. "If you want to move, move."

I raised an eyebrow before taking what she said at face value. I moved, but over her and not away. Our bodies melted together just as perfectly as they had the night before, and if not for wanting to be in the moment, I would have paused to wonder how the fuck it was possible. How was this even more perfect now than it had been before? A part of me had wondered if the glitter of wanting Regina would fade after I'd had her, and now, I had my answer.

"Fuck, I want you again."

Regina laughed before reaching up to wrap her arms around my neck. "Why do you sound so fucking surprised?" She cocked her head to the side as she considered me. "Have you never had an actual relationship?"

"I was in one with you."

"Yeah, but…" She trailed off as she looked at me. "Wow."

"What?"

Regina shifted, and I moved so she could sit up. I watched as she leaned across the bed and opened the drawer to my side table. She pulled out another condom before turning back to me. "Sit up."

I blinked slowly before doing what she asked, sitting with my back against the headboard. She pushed the blankets away, eyes dragging over my body. I sat in silence, letting her get her fill and wondering what she was thinking of as she looked at me. I had been keeping up with my gym routine as a way to also let out some frustration, and it was paying off.

I knew what most women and men thought when they saw me. But Regina had clearly shown that she wasn't like everyone else. I could never actually guess what was going on in her mind, and it kept me on edge and wanting. The worst sort of torture.

"The more you talk, the more I come to realize just how out of the loop you've been," Regina started. She ripped the packet open and pulled out the condom. "At first, I thought you were just fucking with me."

"I told you—"

"I know what you told me," she said, interrupting me with words and actions. My breath hitched when her hands wrapped around my dick, rolling the latex down with no hesitation. "But people lie."

"I wouldn't lie to you."

Regina paused, one hand still around my dick as she looked at me. "No? I don't know if I can say the same."

She shifted then, lifting up on her knees and moving to straddle my thighs.

I shook my head. "I'm not asking you to…promise the same." My words stuttered as she moved, rubbing the head of my dick against the lips of her pussy. I planned to say more, but nothing but a groan left my mouth as she lowered herself, slowly enclosing my dick inside of her without a pause. "Fuck, baby."

Her smirk looked so dirty I couldn't help but flex my hips. I leaned forward, taking one of her nipples between my lips. A hand curled around my head, holding me in place as I lapped at her, drawing that nub in and sucking. When it hardened in my mouth, I pulled back to shift and give its twin the same treatment. Her skin was still salty from the sweat of last night, and I groaned as my mouth filled with spit. I wanted to bite—to take everything from her and give her everything of me.

When Regina lifted and fell again, bouncing in my lap, I hissed and dug my fingers into her hips. A hand shot out, cupping around my throat, and I couldn't stop the thready groan I let out. I let my head fall back against the headboard.

"You really like having my hand around your neck, don't you?"

"Yes." I didn't see reason to lie. My enjoyment of it was obvious, as was hers. "You like it too."

Her eyes narrowed, but she didn't deny it. None of this had been even alluded to when we fell into bed together years ago. Then again, neither of us knew much of anything then. I was still letting my pride lead me astray and posturing.

"Safe word?"

I blinked slowly before replying, "Legacy." Even saying it myself had me wanting to wrinkle my nose in annoyance. It was a word I'd heard thrown around far too often and now it was like fucking kryptonite.

Regina's snort sounded knowing, but she said nothing more. She squeezed softly, not cutting off my breathing but reminding me her grip could change at any time. I didn't know why I liked it so much. No, that was a lie. If anyone else tried it, I'd probably knock them out. But it was her, so she was allowed. She was wanted. I wanted to give her the control. I wanted someone else to make the decisions for a moment and give me a goddamn break from the responsibility of always being the one to hold shit together. Her grip combined with her cunt rubbing over the head of my shaft as she rose and fell had me hardening even more, and I used my hold to help her move.

It was different moving together in the light compared to the night. Last night could have been chalked up to the wine and the mood. This was all us, me biting and her biting back.

"Fuck, you take me so good," I groaned, smacking her ass and enjoying the way it jiggled under my hand. "Perfect."

Her hand tightened at my neck, sending another jolt of arousal through my body. "I know I am. But I'm glad you recognize that." I snorted but couldn't help but agree with her. Nothing got me as hard as Regina not wilting at my words but instead snapping back and giving as good if not better than she got. "Now, fuck me harder."

I shifted and brought my legs up, pressing my feet against the bed so I could thrust up each time she fell against me. Regina's mouth parted on a gasp, and my gaze locked on, glutting myself on every move she made. My hunger for her was unmatched, and I could almost taste her pleasure on the back of my tongue. I brought one hand up to cup her breast, thumbing over her nipple before twisting it between my fingers.

"Want to see you come," I grunted out as our movements grew frenzied. The tops of my thighs began to sing with each slap of Regina's descent. I could feel my balls rising with the need to come, but I pushed it down. I wanted to see her fall apart on top of me. I moved my hand from her hip to feel where we were joined. "Take it, Regina. Fucking make yourself come on my dick."

I slipped my thumb between the hair around her cunt and felt for her clit. When her body jerked, grip spasming at my throat, I snapped up, clasping the back of her neck as I feasted from her mouth. I thrust my tongue in, mirroring my dick inside of her, and reveled in the burst of sound that jumped from her mouth into mine. Her thighs tightened and I had to let go, jerking my hips up as I emptied myself into her.

The air was hot as we fell back against the headboard, sharing rapid breaths back and forth between our still-connected mouths. I knew I would need to get up and make my way into the office eventually, but for now, I had nowhere I would rather be.

~*~*~

I stared at my calendar. Maybe if I looked long enough, it would tell me something different.

"Did you forget about it?" Gregory asked, drawing my attention back to him. He was perched in the chair across from me, pen held in his hand poised over paper as he waited for me to speak. I had tried to get him to use the tablet I bought him for keeping track of things, but he always said he hated writing things down digitally.

Something about the scratch of pen and paper helping lock things in his memory. If not for the fact he had the mind of a steel trap, I would have said that was bullshit. "You were invited as the speaker for your work with the—"

"I remember," I bit out, cutting him off. When he arched an eyebrow at me and pursed his lips, I backtracked a bit. "My apologies. I didn't mean to snap at you."

He narrowed his eyes for a moment before nodding slightly. "You have been out of sorts for a couple days," he said, looking me up and down, or as much as he could from across the desk. "What is going on with you?"

I ran a hand across my face. What was going on with me? It's like the moment I had a taste of Regina, I was unable to think of anything but her. Work was never fun, but it hadn't been this grueling in a long time. I wanted to call her and find a place we could have lunch so I could gorge myself on the taste of her again. It was unnerving to be led around by my dick when I should be putting all my focus into carrying this company across the line and into its successful future—a future that required me keeping up appearances and attending events that continued to garner us goodwill and press.

"Nothing."

"Uh-huh. Try that again," Gregory countered. "It's my job to keep you on track, and I can't do that if you're distracted and I have no idea why. Though…I could probably guess, given the whispers I've heard."

Damn people and their need for gossip. "I can't begin to know what you mean."

His expression was unimpressed, and with anyone else, I would've told them to fuck off. But Gregory was one of the few people I wasn't related to that I could call a friend. He and his husband Alexis were usually my go-to people when I needed to talk things out. Besides the fact that they had no connections with anyone who were a threat to my family, neither of them had any desire to. I paid Gregory well, and Alexis was just too nice of a person. I was sure he could be pushed to be ruthless if needed, but he seemed to save that for their adopted brood of kids.

"Should I tell your trainer you need a second leg day?"

"Leg day was—" I cut myself off when he cocked his head at me. There was a threat there, and only the ache in my legs kept me from calling his bluff. "Fine. It's about Regina."

He nodded. "I figured it was. Things not going as well as you'd hoped?"

I shook my head. "We had sex. Twice."

"Well, okay then," he replied with a smile. "That is some progress, given how business-like you both started this. But sex does not make a relationship. Give me more."

I leaned back in my chair with a soft groan. "The problem is I don't have more to give. I promised to make things up to her, and she's accepted my proposal for the olive branch it is, but she still looks at me like she's waiting for me to strike."

Gregory shrugged. "I mean, can you blame her?" When I protested, he shook his head. "I know you and that you want to make things work with her, but remember, all she has thought of for the past few years is how royally your father fucked her family over and that you were part of that, however unwilling."

He was right, even if I didn't want to admit it. "I told her I would help her in whatever way I can."

"That's great, but are you actively looking to help or are you passively sitting back and waiting for her to come to you?"

That was an angle I hadn't thought about. I was so busy trying not to overstep that I hadn't thought how she might take it if I just waited and did nothing in the interim. Did she see me as passively doing nothing?

"Looks to me like you need to think about how to act instead of giving lip service. I doubt she will trust anything you say unless you put that into action."

I nodded and shifted forward to rest my chin on the back of my hands. "I can see that. But I have to be careful in how I do this. She's already told me to butt out and not try to take charge." Which was hard enough for me to do. I had been in charge for so long I wasn't sure I knew how to play assist. That wasn't a position I was prepared for growing up. But if there was one thing I was good at, it was working around difficult people.

"You're right," I replied with a nod. I knew what my next steps needed to be. "Make sure the organization knows I need a plus-one for the invite. Throw in a couple extra thousand if anyone makes noise about the change."

Gregory smiled before he stood up. "Good luck."

I waited until he closed the door behind him before I picked up my cell and made a call.

"A call during the middle of the day? Things must be going slow over there." Hearing Regina's voice only reinforced how much I wanted to see her, even if it had been less than twenty-four hours since she was last in my arms.

"There's a gala I'm invited to this weekend, and I think you should join me." She didn't reply immediately, though I knew she'd heard my words. I waited her out, giving her time to process though it was difficult. Normally I had no problem with letting silence lapse between me and whoever I was conversing with. That I felt so differently now about silence was something to think about.

"Is there a reason why I should beyond our agreement?"

"It'll be a controlled launch of our relationship. With others more concerned about the event and being seen, it should keep the invasive questioning to a minimum if only for propriety's sake." That was true enough. We wouldn't be the only ones who had used a targeted event to launch a partnership. It was a strategy many of my acquaintances had deployed before. "It's also to benefit charities that I know your father contributed to previously. You might be able to reignite a business relationship with them."

Regina hummed softly. "I see you've been doing your research. Good." It was a backhanded compliment, but I took it with grace. "What time will we need to meet?"

"I'll have the car pick you up around six." She didn't reply, but I could practically hear the gears turning inside her head. "If you need, I can have Gregory contact several boutiques and have them prepare a few looks for you in advance."

"What makes you think I need help looking good?" she asked, voice going even.

"I have no doubt you'll look amazing in anything you wear," I replied carefully. "I only mean to provide you the opportunity to go shopping on my dime."

"And you get what out of that? Are there going to be hidden cameras somewhere that I need to be worried about?"

"If I want to get you on camera, I'll ask. I'd much rather see you disrobe as it is, though that'll require your agreement." I smirked, thinking about the last time she had bared herself for my gaze. I'd almost wanted to ask her to put her clothes on and take them off again just so I could see each inch of her skin unwrapped like a present all my own. "Consent is a big thing with me, Regina. And in all honesty, I would love to hear it from you over and over again in as many positions as we both can stand."

She was quiet again, and I wished I knew exactly what was going through her mind. What I wouldn't give to be able to see inside her thoughts and give her everything she wanted. It wasn't a selfless concept. I got just as much enjoyment at seeing her find joy as I did finding my own.

Voyeur. It was a term I had heard batted around more than once, and I suppose here it fit. I knew that Regina would no doubt find pleasure in seeing the Dummond name go down in flames, and if not for what that would mean for my siblings and my mother, I probably would have let whatever she planned be carried out with little to no interference from me.

Maybe I should have a little more self-preservation, but the Dummond name had caused us enough grief over the years that if I could, I would rip it down and start anew.

"Fine. Send your lackey. If you want me to spend your dad's blood money, I will."

"Gregory isn't my lackey," I corrected. "He's my friend and a good person who had no dealings with my dad. Not everyone around me is like him, Regina. I was serious about changing things, and I will prove it to you for the rest of my life if I have to."

I didn't expect my words to move her, but I could only hope Gregory was right about what I needed to plan next.

Chapter Sixteen

Regina

Jonathan's words had been achingly sincere two days ago when he mentioned wanting to dress me for this gala. When I had said yes, I don't know what I was expecting, but it wasn't for a car to appear in front of my condo, complete with a bottle of champagne and a dozen roses. The man who had been driving stepped out, coming around and opening the door for me. When I approached, another man who I recognized as Gregory from the picture Jonathan sent me, was already seated in the back.

I paused for a moment, wondering if I were being utterly foolish to get in a car with two men I didn't know to go to a gala I hadn't originally been invited to. There was probably a public service announcement somewhere about this very thing. Gregory smiled catching my attention.

"Hi Regina. Jonathan sent me along to ensure you have the best experience possible." His voice wasn't particularly deep, but it had a strangely soothing quality to it. "I figured it would be easier for me to get to know you and what you like if I talked to you instead of just silently driving you around."

I nodded as I let myself be herded into the car. Right when I sat down, my phone pinged, and I opened it to see a message from Jonathan.

'Gregory is your guide for the afternoon. I called ahead to the boutiques and let them know money is no object. See you tonight.'

I stared at the text for a moment as the car pulled away from the curb. I knew the man was loaded, but I didn't really think he was going to say the sky was the limit. Clearly, he was pulling out the big guns, but for what? Just so I would forgive him? It didn't make sense for the man he was known to be.

"Do you have a preference for which boutique to check out first?"

I frowned and tried to remember the last time I needed something dressy enough for a gala. I didn't often go to those back in London, preferring to keep a lower profile and handle things on the business front instead of rubbing elbows. My mom was heads and shoulders above me at that. Her personality had people spilling secrets before they even realized it. I tried to emulate some of that ability, but my skills were more on the planning and research side. I could follow a thread for miles, but I was shit at making it appear in the first place.

"Whichever you suggest," I replied as I sat back. I watched the buildings go by as I tried to think of how this would all play out. I had told Christa about attending the gala with Jonathan, and she had been giddy as a damn schoolgirl about having someone else there to talk to. Honestly, knowing she would be there also gave me a small measure of relief. "Did Jonathan have a color in mind for me?"

"Not in the slightest," Gregory replied, amusement clear in his tone. "In fact, he told me to allow you to dictate the color scheme for the evening and he would match."

I turned to him not sure if I had heard him right. "He's letting me choose. Are you having me on right now?" He laughed and shook his head. I was surprised that someone so seemingly open was an assistant for Jonathan's surly ass. "You're not who I pictured working with Jonathan."

He arched an eyebrow. "Oh? Let me guess. You figured he'd have someone super serious who spoke in grunts and glares?"

Despite my reservations, I chuckled and nodded. "Pretty much. He always was so serious even when we were younger. Maybe even more so." I could concede that the

Jonathan of the present was far less reserved and grim than I thought he would be. The memory of his face slack-jawed in pleasure filled my mind, and I had to uncross my legs and cross them again. Lord knows I didn't need to be thinking of him coming while I was in the company of others.

"He is still far too serious sometimes for someone in their thirties, but I suppose when you have to deal with all the bullshit that comes with a well-known name, it'll do that to you."

We lapsed into silence as the car continued through the crowded Atlanta streets. I wasn't sure what Gregory was thinking, but my mind was filled with unwanted what-ifs—the kind that I had no business thinking. When the car pulled into a parking lot, I looked up and was surprised. The boutique was small and out of the way, but the styled mannequins in the window were the star of the show. I had been expecting gaudy monstrosities that would swamp me in material and weigh me down, but the gowns were on another level.

Simple. Understated. Elegant. Everything I preferred when it came to dressing myself. It was the type of style I fought my mom on to this day. I followed Gregory inside, nodding hello to the saleswoman who greeted us. Before long, we were seated on plush couches and both handed a glass of champagne.

"Mr. Dummond has provided us with your measurements, so you can rest assured that anything you choose can be tailored and readied for wear this evening."

I nodded before letting my gaze scan the racks of couture. I was surprised to see the fabric laid perfectly over curves in ways that were often tough to find at this price point. Truthfully, I had expected to have to pull something out of my own closet and doctor it up. Despite my best effort, I felt another wall between Jonathan and me fall.

"See anything you like?"

"Too many," I replied, casting a small smile toward Gregory. He looked perfectly at home perched on the couch beside me with a flute held delicately between his fingers. I took a moment to really look at him. He was older than me, based on the faint smile lines around his eyes. His brown hair was dusted with grays, and he was heavyset in a way that was more intimidating than anything. When he glanced my way, his brown eyes were kind with still a bit of lingering amusement.

"You have a question?"

"Just curious about you and how you started working for Jonathan," I answered truthfully. He didn't raise any alarm bells for me, so I relaxed a fraction. He smiled before gesturing for me to stand and leading me to a row of gowns that I had been eyeing since we walked in. It wasn't until I had chosen a few and was behind the curtain being helped into the first one that he spoke again.

"I met Jonathan about nine years ago when I interviewed to be an assistant for his father." I paused my motions and wondered if I had been lulled into a false sense of security with this man. Anyone who would willingly deal with the senior Dummond was someone instantly on my shit list. "Of course, I hadn't known how much of a bastard the man was initially until he heard that I had a husband instead of a wife and acted like I had propositioned him in the middle of the damn boardroom."

That wasn't a surprising statement, given Jameson's history. "How did that translate to you working for his son?" I asked as I walked out from behind the curtain. The dress was a deep mauve with a flatteringly low neckline and a cinched waist that had my curves on full display. It was cute, but I wasn't about to just choose the first one I saw.

Gregory nodded appreciatively. "That color looks amazing next to your complexion." I looked over my shoulder into the mirror. He wasn't wrong and we both knew it. "Maybe too understated for the coming out event tonight, but definitely good to have in your closet for later."

I agreed before walking back into the dressing area and moving on to the next. The lady helping me smiled before making quick work of the hidden clasps at my back.

"Jonathan was in that meeting and gave his father an earful. Granted, no voices were raised, but with what I know about him now, it was akin to a shouting match," Gregory said. "After that, he walked me out and offered me a job working for him. Later, I learned that his brother had just been shipped off somewhere after their dad found him in a very compromising position with another man, so I'm assuming that had something to do with it."

I couldn't help but smile at that. Petty was damn near my middle name, and I lived for the fact that Jonathan stuck it to his dad about his homophobic bullshit. "I hope you gave the man the stink eye every time you saw him."

Gregory laughed as I came back around the curtain in the next dress. "Even better, I brought my husband to the Christmas party and kissed him under the mistletoe where that bastard had a clear view. His expression made my little gay heart sing."

I grinned sharply. "Gregory, I think you and I are going to get along just fine."

His eyes glinted as he smiled back. "Please, call me Greg."

~*~*~

I didn't know why the hell I was nervous. A glance in the full-length mirror in my foyer showed just how perfect I looked. I had gone with a ruby red off-the-shoulder gown with lace embellishments and a sweetheart neckline. My pearl earrings had small diamonds that matched my bracelet. Luckily, the dress itself had only needed a few minor adjustments. The other dresses I chose would be delivered in the next few weeks, and I had thanked Greg profusely for convincing me that spending the money was worth it, especially on someone else's dime.

"The man can afford it. If he wants to pay, let him pay."

He was right. If this was part of Jonathan groveling at my feet, then I was going to let myself enjoy it. My cell rang, and I jumped slightly before grabbing it off the coffee table.

"Mom? What are you doing awake at this hour?" I glanced at the clock. "It's almost eleven."

"You didn't think I would let you go to that event without giving you a call, did you? FaceTime me so I can see you."

I sighed softly but did as she asked before holding the phone further away from me. When she came on the screen, I couldn't help but smile. While Casey favored our dad in so many ways, I was the spitting image of our mom. We had the same full lips, the same shaggy eyebrows that meant regular waxing appointments, and the same nose.

"Oh, honey, you look amazing." I smiled before turning the camera away so she could see me in the mirror. "That dress is absolutely perfect on you. I'm so glad to see you out of a suit."

I rolled my eyes at the soft dig but didn't let it deter me. I knew she meant well, even if it was annoying. "Thanks, mom."

"And you're sure about this? Going with Jonathan and being—"

"Ma, we talked about this," I insisted. "He's apologized for his father's actions, and he's done nothing but go above and beyond to make amends." It wasn't a lie. He was going full throttle on his apology tour, but I didn't need her to worry about me. I wasn't giving in that easily. He was still going to have to work harder.

"I know," she replied. "But honey, you don't know how bad things could get when dealing with a Dummond. One minute they're on your side and the next—"

The call box rang, cutting off her sentence. I was grateful to it. I didn't want to have to spend more time assuring her I knew what I was getting myself into when I wasn't even sure of how things were playing out myself. Never mind the fact that I hadn't yet come clean about our supposed engagement. Then there was the problem of having fallen into bed with the man after only a couple weeks. No. The less she knew, the better.

"Mom, the car is here."

"Oh, alright. Call me when you get home and please be careful. If he does anything, I will call your uncle and have him come straight over there. He doesn't mind going back to prison."

Fucking hell. I had to force myself to nod and agree just to get her off the phone. Threats of maiming aside, I knew she was right about a lot of things. I hadn't shared all of my plans with either of my parents before leaving, only that I was coming back to try my hand at building the business back up in Atlanta. They hadn't been excited about it, but I was an adult now and they trusted me. I wondered how long that would last when Jonathan and I did go public with our engagement. It was a problem for another day. Tonight, I had to have my game face on.

A soft knock on the door surprised me, and I glanced in the peephole before opening the door.

Jonathan stood there, hand poised to knock again. His beard was trimmed neatly close to his face and his skin looked smooth and glowy. Wide shoulders were draped in the soft-looking fabric of his tuxedo, and he had a bowtie that matched the color of my dress. In his other hand, he held a bouquet of blood-red roses. When I met his gaze, the fire there nearly had me sweating. He licked his lips, drawing my attention to them. Time stopped as we stood there, eyes on one another, and I wondered if I had just made a terrible mistake.

Chapter Seventeen

Jonathan

Fuck.

That was the only thought in my mind as I stared at the literal goddess in front of me. I had known the gown Regina chose thanks to Gregory's text, but his description hadn't prepared me for seeing it on her. Regina could have commanded armies or had men worshipping at her feet, and she was going to be on my arm. I didn't know who I had to thank for this, but they had my eternal gratitude.

"You're beautiful." It was an understatement, but I found myself at a loss for more words to describe the vision that was her. When she smiled, my heart damn near skipped a beat, and I covered my silence by holding out the flowers to her. "I brought these for you."

"I figured as much," she said with a teasing lilt to her voice. She reached out to get them and our fingers brushed, sending a pulse of tantalizing heat through me. I watched her as she walked into her condo before slowly stepping across the threshold.

I didn't know what I was expecting. Interior decorating wasn't my forte, and I had relied on a hired decorator for my own properties. The ceilings were high, making the space feel airy even in the foyer. When I walked around the corner, I was greeted by a wall of windows showcasing the Atlanta skyline. I paused when I saw Regina walk back into the living room holding a vase full of water.

"Let me help you with that," I said, moving quickly toward her. She smiled up at me, and I nearly dropped the vase as she handed it over. That was the first time she had smiled at me so openly, and I wanted to see it again. I tore my eyes away to fiddle with the flowers, getting the stems inside and sighing when they tried to fight back.

"Never thought I would see the day when you struggle with anything," Regina joked. I glanced at her, and that same grin was still on her face as she watched me fight with Mother Nature.

"You could help me out."

"Not a chance in hell," she said with a soft snort. I shook my head but couldn't stop myself from smiling slightly. I heard the sound of a shutter click but ignored it when I finally got the final stem stuffed in the hole. I made a triumphant noise and took a step back. The roses looked beautiful against the backdrop of waning light. I wasn't sure where she had put the ones I sent with the car earlier, but I would worry about that later when I wasn't so greedy to catch sight of her smile.

Her lips were painted an attractive ruby, matching her dress, and I swallowed hard at the thought of smudging that color until there was nothing left. When her gaze met mine, she cocked her head to the side.

"What?"

Telling her the depraved thoughts running through my mind right then was probably not the best bet. Instead, I took a gamble and reached my arm out toward her. "Nothing. Are you ready to go?"

Regina glanced down for a moment before slowly curling her arm around mine. She had a shawl and small clutch in her other hand, and before she could ask, I reached for them, leaving her hands free. She raised an eyebrow at me but followed as I led her back to the front door.

"Are you planning on walking around with my purse in your hand?"

I looked down at it before shrugging. "I think it looks quite fetching with my bowtie."

Her giggle had me giddy. It was a struggle for me to be this light with anyone else. It had been one of father's annoyances with me—my inability to charm. That was Jameson's, or even more so, Jerome's domain. Women young and old loved to talk with them, and they could hold their attention like no other. It was something that had frustrated me when I was younger, but slowly I learned that my strengths lay in other areas. But now, I wanted to be able to hold Regina's attention. Having her eyes on me and me alone was a heady feeling I craved.

"I suppose so," she replied, eyeing me.

Walking out of the building with her on my arm had me standing taller than usual. I helped her into the limo before sliding in after her. Once the car was on its way, I opened the bottle of champagne I had gotten after speaking with Gregory. Regina looked over, eyes widening.

"Oh. That's what Greg and I had earlier."

"I know," I replied, pouring her a flute of the bubbly amber liquid. "He told me you enjoyed it and asked the boutique where to find it."

When I handed her the glass, our fingers brushed again, and she favored me with a look over the rim. I didn't know what that look meant, but it sent a shiver through me. I would never give Jameson shit again when he talked to me about McKenzie. Fuck, I was just as bad if not worse than him. I was pretty sure McKenzie hadn't asked him for millions of dollars. Then again, if she had, I doubt my brother would have said no. That made two of us. I had effectively signed that away with the contract and I still felt zero remorse.

"You're awfully quiet. What's going on in that head of yours?"

Her question brought me out of my own thoughts, and I leaned back against the seat. I had talked to Gregory, and he had pushed the idea that if I were going to get Regina to fall for me as sure as I had for her, I would need to be honest. I knew from experience that secrets could break a relationship, no matter how strong the foundation. When it came to Regina, I knew keeping secrets was an even bigger issue. I had to get things right this time.

"Just thinking about how lucky I am that you're giving me a second chance." It wasn't the totality of what was running through my head, but it was a major part of it. I knew now was probably not the best time to be broaching the subject. We were about to be surrounded by people who would be watching our every reaction and trying to find anything they could use to spread gossip. But I was eager to know where she stood with things between us. "I'm glad you decided to join me this evening."

She looked over at me for a moment before shaking her head. "You really are something, Jonnie."

I perked up then. The last time she had called me that, I hadn't yet broken her heart. As if knowing my thoughts, she quickly took a sip of her champagne. I let her be even as warmth bloomed in my chest. Something had shifted between us. I could almost taste it. But like the most elusive of scents, I knew that if I tried to run after it, it would disappear like it never existed. I let the nickname sit between us, heavy with the possibility of what it could mean.

"About that," I started, figuring now was as good a time as any to give her the presents I had prepared. I leaned forward to grab the bag I had hidden in the storage compartment and pulled a rectangular box out before turning and handing it to her.

Regina looked at the box in her hand before looking back up at me. "What is this?"

"A gift for you. One of many." I took her glass and set it to the side so she could open it. When she did, her breath hitched, and she looked up at me sharply. The white gold necklace was two strands of pear-shaped diamonds that I knew would sit perfectly on her neck. When I was searching for the perfect accessories to match her dress, I had been pulled to it, especially with how it matched the other gift I'd already had made for her.

"Jonathan…" Her voice trailed off as she looked back down at the necklace. Before she could refuse it, I reached out and took the box from her. I felt her eyes on me as I undid the clasps and lifted the necklace from its holder.

"Turn, please." She stared at me for a moment before surprisingly doing what I asked with no further comment. I lifted my arms, curling them around in front of her. When the necklace settled on her skin, Regina shivered, and I had to fight against leaning forward to taste that movement against my tongue. Her perfume tonight was heady, and I let it curl around me like a seductive dancer. The clasp was small, and I narrowed my eyes as I forced my fingers to comply in closing it. Once it was done, I couldn't help but brush my thumbs against the back of her neck.

"Can I turn around now?" Regina asked, voice hushed. The car was filled with a delicious sort of tension that had me wanting to see her in the necklace and nothing else. Still, I had one more thing to give her.

"Yes," I answered softly before reaching back into the bag and pulling out a small square box. When her eyes landed on it, I felt time stop. I had never been in this position—giving a ring to anyone. This was new for me, and I found I couldn't treat it flippantly. Regina might not be ready to go all in, but I was.

For me, this wasn't a game.

"Jonathan. You ca—"

"If you show up tonight without a ring on your finger, everyone will talk and not in a good way," I said quickly, heading off her words. I didn't want denials. I didn't care if this was only happening because she had come back with some sort of revenge plot against my fucking father. This ring was a promise, and one I intended to fulfill.

Our gazes locked even as I opened the box to reveal the ring. Normally I didn't care about jewelry beyond the watch father had gifted all us boys years ago, but when I saw this ring, all I could imagine was it sitting on Regina's finger, knowing I had put it there. I carefully removed it and turned to her. Regina's expression didn't change as she looked at me, and I held my breath, wondering if this was going a step too far for her. This ring made our agreement real.

"This is your last chance to back out, no questions asked," I said, giving her an excuse as much as it pained me.

"Jonnie, this isn't real." Her voice was quiet, but I heard her well enough. Still, I remembered Gregory's words. It was all about action. It was about showing her that I was in this, wherever it might take us.

I moved, taking her left hand. "It's real enough for me." Slowly giving her time to change her mind, I slid the emerald bloom ring on her finger, admiring how it shone against her skin. All the air seemed to rush out of me then at the knowledge that I had put a ring on her. There it was, the physical embodiment of our agreement. "People have gotten engaged for far worse reasons, right?"

Regina had been staring down at her hand, but at my words, she looked up at me. Her mouth opened and closed with no sound coming out. Before she could regain her speech, I picked her glass back up and handed it to her. She took it, looking down at it as if she had never seen it before in her life. I clinked my glass with hers.

"To us."

She huffed out soft laughter before her lips twisted into a grin. "To us."

One more glass later and we were being escorted into the Murphy. The ballroom had been transformed into a glittering sphere of wealth and privilege. I saw many familiar faces as we walked in, and some who probably should have been familiar but I couldn't recall. Regina's hand tightened on my arm, and when I turned to look at her, I caught sight of Liam. He was standing with some others I recognized, and he had a petite blonde by his side looking at him adoringly. I almost felt sorry for the woman until she turned away and that expression faded away as if it were never there. I snorted in amusement before my attention was pulled by Jameson and McKenzie walking over to us.

"About time you got here," Jameson said, relief clear in his tone. I pulled away from Regina momentarily to give him a quick hug before stepping back and lightly resting my hand against her. Warmth nearly had me forgetting what I wanted to say, but when she glanced at me, I got my head back in the game. "Jennifer and Jalissa are already seated at the table with mom."

That had me widening my eyes in surprise. Jameson nodded, though his expression soured slightly. I knew I needed to talk to him about that, but now wasn't the time. I turned to Regina and pressed gently on her back.

"I believe you know Regina," I said, reintroducing them before gesturing to McKenzie. "Regina, this is Jameson's fiancée, McKenzie. McKenzie, this is my fiancée, Regina."

McKenzie's smile was wide and open, and I instantly felt more at ease. How Jameson managed to bag someone as sweet as her I would never know, but I appreciated it. She didn't know shit about the business world, nor did she care to. I liked that about her. Plus, she made Jameson happy. As long as she continued to with no ulterior motives, I was fine with it. Then again, I really couldn't throw stones, given my own questionable relationship.

Regina and McKenzie exchanged greetings, and I moved around to let them get acquainted. Jameson took a step beside me.

"So, things seem to be going well," he said as we both looked out over the crowd. A few people were glancing our way, and we nodded in greeting. I knew Regina and I would need to make a circuit around the room to work things in, but I wanted her to feel comfortable first. After this, things would no doubt kick up a notch.

"With you as well," I replied. "Did Jerome bring anyone this time?"

Jameson rolled his eyes. "Do you really think he would be caught looking like a productive member of the family?" I knew that wasn't totally fair. Jerome was good at the work he did, and he was dependable in his own way. But when it came to settling down, he was even worse about it than the rest of us. I wouldn't be surprised if one day he rocked up to the house with a kid in tow before he announced a stable relationship. It was looking like Jameson and McKenzie were mom's best bet for grandchildren anytime soon.

"I guess it's better than the last girl he brought to one of these things. How father kept that out of the gossip mill I will never know." Jameson chuckled but didn't counter my words. When the lights flickered, we both collected our dates and made our way to the table.

Jennifer looked up at us with a raised brow when I pulled out a chair for Regina, but I ignored her. If she had something to say, I knew she would wait until we weren't surrounded by prying eyes and attentive ears. I had filled them in on the coming out of sorts, but this was the first time all of them were coming face-to-face with Regina. For Jerome, it would be the first time he met her at all. When we were all seated, the light glanced off Regina's ring, drawing attention to it.

"Holy hell, bro," Jerome said. "Could you have found a rock any bigger?"

Jameson snickered beside me, and I gave him a look. "Probably," I said before nodding to Regina. "If she decides she wants a bigger one, I will."

Regina looked at me before shaking her head. "Any bigger and my damn finger would break off. Besides," she said, looking at it with a soft smile, "I like it. It suits me."

I watched her, feeling another part of me loosen at her obvious enjoyment. I didn't think she was lying. Her expression looked too damn pleased to be faked.

"Oh my god. Are you smiling, Jonnie?" I scowled at Jalissa's words. She was looking at me with a wide smile, and even Jennifer looked pleased. "No, no. I'm sorry. Bring back the smile. Regina, can you look at him or something so he stops looking like a constipated asshole?"

Regina laughed, and I tried to keep my scowl on my face, but fuck was it hard. Clearly, I was going to have to make sure she and Jalissa stayed as far from one another as possible. Regina was absolutely the type to enjoy when my sister tried to get a rise out of me.

"I'll do my best," she said before placing her hand on mine. I turned my hand over to thread our fingers together, and when I felt my lips twitch, I forced myself to look toward the stage and ignore my siblings, who were no doubt still talking shit at my expense. Still, it was worth it when Regina's hand squeezed mine slightly.

Chapter Eighteen

Regina

The night should have been uncomfortable, what with meeting Jonathan's family and putting our relationship on the map with his associates. But with the weight of the necklace on my chest and the ring on my finger, I found myself annoyingly at ease. Watching him scowl as his siblings took the piss out of him was delightful, and I found myself laughing more than I had in the weeks since I had moved back. Somehow, I had found myself integrated into the one family I thought I hated, and I wasn't even fucking sure how it happened.

How was this real life?

"Are you alright?"

I turned toward Mrs. Dummond. Somehow, I had ended up seated next to her, though I wasn't sure if that had been purposeful or just the way things happened. Her dark brown eyes weren't as warm as McKenzie's, but she still seemed sincere in her concern. I gave her a small smile.

"I am. I'm still adjusting to being back after so many years," I replied, keeping my tone light. I didn't know how much she knew about my history with her family. Given how little Jonathan seemed to know, I wondered if it was the same for her. Did she know about the hell her husband had put my family through? Did she condone it? I was aggravatingly eager to know if the marriage she'd had was as surface-level as my own engagement with her son.

No, that wasn't totally right. There was something there bubbling just on the fringes between Jonathan and me. It was the same thing that had me impulsively reaching for his hand under the table. It was the same thing that I didn't want to look too closely at. I tried to focus back on Mrs. Dummond and not my own traitorous thoughts or the man at my side.

"I remember you, you know," she said softly, her voice not carrying beyond me hopefully. The words were targeted for me, and I tried to school my expression to not show how shocked I was at that. "Your mother was a good friend for many years until…"

Her voice trailed off, but I knew exactly what she meant. Until her husband decided the partnership no longer suited him. "I wasn't sure if any of you would remember me. It's been so long."

"It's not every day your son falls in love," she replied with a nod. I knew she wasn't nodding at me, though. She was gesturing toward Jonathan. "Ten years, and yet as soon as you're back in town, he searches you out."

She had to be mistaken. Love? Jonathan hadn't sought me out. If anything, I had come to him, right? I wanted to be angry at her for stirring up these needless questions, but when she smiled and patted me on the hand, seeming so much like my own mother, I froze with indecision. A part of me wanted to fight back and deny it, but another part of me blossomed at the thought of it all. Lust was one thing, but love?

"He is not his father."

That brought me out of my thoughts as I focused on her again. Brown eyes looked at me knowingly, and I had to fight to meet them head-on. "Ma'am?"

"Jonnie," Mrs. Dummond reiterated. "No matter what people say, he is not like his father. He cares. Truly. And he wants to be better. I think losing you made him want to be better."

Before I could respond, the lights dimmed, and the program began. As I sat under the cover of darkness, her words continued to circle in my mind. Never would I think someone would use me as a moral compass. But she had spoken so surely as if she knew without a shadow of a doubt her words rang true.

"Is everything alright?" Jonathan whispered into my ear. I turned my head, startled at how close we were. His face was right there, close enough we could almost share the same breath. The lights from the stage illuminated him enough that I could see the concern in his gaze. Without thinking, I leaned forward and brushed my lips over his. The soft hitch of breath from him let me know how surprised he was by my forwardness. I was too, honestly. I wanted to say it was a calculated move to show our relationship to the public, but really, I just wanted to.

I wanted to kiss him.

With a hum, Jonathan leaned forward, pressing a second kiss to my lips, keeping it light enough to be polite. He smiled softly before covering my hand again. When applause started around us, I blinked quickly, wondering what the hell I had missed. Jonathan flashed a smile before standing. I frowned slightly as I walked him walk over to the stage. I had missed whatever was going on, but I made sure to dutifully clap along with everyone else.

Jonathan stood on stage, looking at home in front of an audience. His smile was wide, but I could tell it was forced. As at home as he looked to anyone else, it was a shock to realize I could read his true feelings on his face. His voice was even as he said his speech, thanking everyone for the award and the chance to work with them, but underneath, I could hear the strain. He was more comfortable in his office making plans than being front and center receiving recognition, that much was clear.

"He always did hate being put on display," Mrs. Dummond muttered. I saw one of Jonathan's sisters nod in agreement.

"I'm surprised he didn't ask Jameson to accept the honor for him."

Jameson chuckled. "He did. I turned him down." When we looked at him in surprise, he shrugged. "You act like I would want to be up there. He's the big man in charge. He can handle it."

I snorted and shook my head as their other sister quietly laid into him. McKenzie caught my eye and shook her head with a smile. I gave her one of my own as amusement filled me. When Jonathan sat back down at the table, I reached for his hand. Part of it was because I knew people were watching, but mostly I just wanted to. I leaned over to him.

"Good job."

"Thanks. I still don't know what the fuck this award is for," he replied, whispering like it was a big secret to keep. I snorted before turning my attention back to the stage as more awards were announced. It was a boring but necessary part of doing business, and I knew I needed to build up my tolerance to them because I would be attending a lot more as Jonathan's plus-one.

At least the food is good, I mused as the lights were turned back on and the dinner service began. Slowly, conversation filled the air along with the sounds of cutlery and twinkling glasses. I didn't know how Jonathan had managed to get me on the invite list at such short notice, but it probably had something to do with dollar signs. After our plates had been cleared away with more than one glass of wine, Jonathan stood up and offered his hand to me.

"May I have this dance?"

I glanced around the room and realized some people had begun dancing to the band's soft music. Conversation around the table had been surprisingly easy, but I knew we still needed to launch this relationship in earnest. Mind made up, I let him pull me to standing, and we made our way to the dance floor.

Some couples were slow dancing with eyes only for one another, and I felt a little envy. What it must be like, to have a relationship like that? I had never allowed myself to think about what it must be like because it had never been in the cards for me. I was married to my work and my revenge. Or…I had been.

My work was still just as important, but my revenge had practically been dead on arrival. My grand plan of having the people who snubbed my family pay for their transgressions hadn't gone anywhere. The Boldens were assholes but untouchable by me, and Jonathan's dad had fucked back off to hell before I even got here. That left me with a blank sheet of nothing. All that was left was the business.

"Is everything alright?"

It was hilarious how similar Jonathan was to his mom with that same question. I nodded as I lifted my hands up to settle on his shoulders. We moved together in unspoken agreement, swaying side to side to the soft beat. Jonathan's hands were settled at my waist, branding heat against me through the soft fabric of my gown. How the man radiated so much warmth I would never understand.

"I'm fine," I replied before glancing around us. My gaze landed on Christa, and when she saw me, she waved. I smiled and gave her a small wave back, though I had forgotten there was a big difference between now and the last time she saw me. When her eyes widened, I frowned, confused what had brought on that change. "Christa is coming over here."

Jonathan frowned before turning to look behind him. Right when she got to us, we slowed our movements.

"Oh my gosh, girl! Do you have a little announcement you want to tell us?"

I blinked quickly, trying to pinpoint what she meant. "What are you talking about? I saw you like two days ago."

She gave me a look. "Exactly. Two days ago, you didn't have that on your finger." When she pointed at my hand, I looked down and remembered the ring. Other than Jerome's initial outburst, no one else in Jonathan's family had really remarked on it, so I had forgotten it was there.

"Oh," I said as I quickly thought of something to say. Jonathan saved me by wrapping an arm around my waist.

"We do have an announcement, actually," he replied before turning to look at me. "I asked Regina to marry me, and she graciously accepted."

Christa practically squealed, causing several people to look our way. Before I could say anything, I was wrapped in a hug.

"Congratulations!" Her joy was palpable, and I smiled, nodding my thanks. "Jonathan is so much better of a match than Liam."

"I believe so too," Jonathan said. He pressed a kiss against the side of my head, and I leaned into it without thinking. How was it that being like this with him had become so easy?

Christa was almost vibrating in her excitement, and she reached out and grabbed my hand. "Okay, as much as I know you don't want to be separated from her, I need to introduce her to some people."

I looked helplessly at Jonathan, but all he did was nod. Being amongst the masses and having to engage in small talk was not my idea of a good time, but still, I let Christa pull me away towards a group of other women. Making connections was important, and it was the reason I had agreed to this in the first place. I glanced back at Jonathan, wondering why he didn't move as I was dragged away.

An hour later, I was wishing he had protested. Christa turned out to seemingly know everyone at the gala and was gleeful about taking me to meet them. The good news was I had a couple meetings on my calendar for real estate. The bad news was I was sure I had a bunion on my pinky toe. It took a few minutes before I could excuse myself to the bathroom, but when I finally found my way into a stall, I let out a sigh of relief. Peopling was hard, but I knew it would be worth it in the end. Right when I was finishing up, the door opened, and I could hear several voices. I was about to flush and leave when my name was mentioned.

"I can't believe out of everyone, Jonathan decided on an engagement with *her*. I mean, who the hell is Regina to begin with?" I frowned at the unfamiliar voice but had to focus as another one spoke up.

"I heard her father went bankrupt and now she's after his wealth." I had to keep myself from snorting. Whoever it was wasn't totally off. I just found it funny they acted like that wasn't something people did every day. "Marigold saw her having lunch with Christa last week. I should probably tell Christa not to associate with people like that. Ever since she started dating that guy Marco, she's been running with the wrong crowd."

"I thought his name was Marcello?"

The women's voices dissolved into giggles until I heard the bathroom door open again.

"Oh, Melania. Good to see you." I frowned at the thought of someone else joining rather than them leaving. "Are you enjoying the gala?"

"I was until Jonathan came in with some no-name skank." I had to clench my teeth to keep myself from launching out of the stall. "I can't believe he broke our engagement and not even a year later, he's engaged to someone else."

The other women made sounds of agreement, but all I could think about was the fact that Jonathan had been engaged before. In all our conversations, I didn't remember him talking about that at all. We had discussed engagements, but not the fact that he had been in one. Or more.

"Are you going to talk to him about it?"

"I should. I mean, we were together for three years. That is a long time for a relationship."

Murmurs answered her, but the sounds died down as the women left the restroom. I waited until the room was completely quiet before flushing the toilet and walking out. Somehow, I had obtained more information during this bathroom break than I had in the weeks since my first run-in with Jonathan. I stared at the ring on my finger and wondered if his words were all a lie. Had I gotten a hand-me-down engagement ring?

And why the fuck did it matter to me so much if I had?

Chapter Nineteen

Jonathan

The ride back to Regina's was quiet, but I let it be. The night had gone well, and surprisingly, I hadn't hated being around all those people like I usually did. There were some comments here and there congratulating Regina and me on our engagement as well as a few side-eyes I couldn't bother to give a shit about, but overall, I thought the relationship launch was a huge success. Seeing my mother out and about was also a relief. I had caught bits and pieces of her conversation with Regina, but when nothing looked amiss, I'd left it alone.

I couldn't get a sense of how Regina felt about this first foray into publicity. She had been quiet for most of the evening, but I knew she, like me, wasn't big into those types of events. She had smiled when needed and never shied away from my touch, though I kept things light no matter how much I wanted to hold her close and not let go. Christa had been there and was a great help in getting Regina talking to some people. I hadn't asked, but I hoped she would feel free to come to me as needed. There was a fine line between helping and overstepping, and I was being careful not to cross it.

When the limo slowed to a stop in front of her building, I got out, quickly waving off the driver's attempts. I opened Regina's door and reached out to help her from the car. Her hand in mine—just that small touch was intoxicating, and I tried not to seem too forward in hoping I would be invited up. Just because we'd had sex once didn't mean she wanted to do it again, and I wasn't sure how to even ask. How the fuck I managed to get into anyone's pants was a mystery to me at this fucking point.

"I hope tonight wasn't too much for you," I said as I walked her to the building's entrance. "I don't often attend these types of events."

She snorted softly beside me before turning to look up at me. "Let me guess, you send Jameson instead?"

I nodded. "I do. He at least finds them entertaining, and people tend to like him more than me." I pulled the door open for her and followed her, trying not to be so obvious in my enjoyment of how well her gown hugged her from behind. "People find me too similar to our father for comfort at times."

It was a bit of honesty I hadn't told anyone else outside of Gregory. It was an unwanted legacy to be the living reminder of the man who might have fucked you over. Some couldn't separate me from my father, and that was just something I was learning to deal with. There wasn't much I could do about it other than plastic surgery, and that was extreme on a completely different level.

I offered my arm to Regina again, just as amazed as before when she took it. Her heels let out loud clacks against the marbled lobby floor, and when we reached the elevators, we both paused and turned to look at one another. Her dark brown eyes were unfathomable, and I desperately wished I knew what she was thinking.

"I suppose tonight wasn't completely terrible," she said, finally smiling when I chuckled. She pressed the button, and I tried not to think about how it would feel to have her hands on me again. It seemed that everything she did was designed to set my blood on fire despite my best efforts. "At least Liam got a look at what he missed out on."

Her words had something twisting in me. The thought of her considering Liam at all had me wanting to wipe any trace of the man from her mind. It was an irrational desire built upon arousal and a jealousy I probably had no right to feel. Still, I couldn't help but never want to hear that name ever fall from her lips again.

"If he'd had you, I doubt he would even know what to do with you," I bit out as we waited for the elevator. I could feel Regina's gaze on me, but I stared straight ahead, trying to calm my annoyance at being reminded of his existence. I would be happy enough to never hear his name again.

The elevator door opened, and I followed Regina in. When we turned, I saw her still watching me. I glanced over at her, wondering if she was going to speak or let me stew in my thoughts for the ride up to her place. I wasn't assuming I would be let in, but I insisted on walking her to her door at the very least. I might have been a bastard to some, but I was still raised to be a gentleman.

The tension in the elevator had me on edge. She had dropped my arm when we stepped in, and now we stood with only a couple inches of bare air separating us. I wanted to reach across that divide, but I held back, trying to feel her out.

"You seemed to find your stride talking with people," I said as the elevator car started its slow ascent. "Anything interesting business-wise that I can help with? Help. Not take over."

Her mouth clicked shut with my last words, and I quirked my lips up at her. She hummed but didn't break my gaze. "I have a couple luncheons scheduled for next week. If—and that is a big if—I need your assistance, I will let you know."

I nodded in agreement. "Fair enough. I won't interfere."

"You say that now," she taunted. The doors dinged and opened on her floor before I could counter her words. I didn't think I was that damn overbearing and said as much. Regina gave me a look when we reached her door. "Just by watching you with your siblings, I can tell you that you are the most Mother Hen-ing ass person I have ever been around."

That was news to me. "You're the only one who thinks so," I assured her confidently. Her laughter was not what I expected, and I frowned. "Why are you laughing?"

"Because you're so clueless it's almost adorable," she replied before unlocking her door. She stepped through the doorway before pausing and looking at me over her shoulder. "Well? Do you need a handwritten invitation?"

"Explicit consent, remember?"

Her gaze slowly traveled up and down my body, lighting me up, and I made an aborted move toward her. Her lips curled up in a smirk. "Is that so?" She walked back toward me, hips swaying to a beat only she could hear, and I stood almost frozen in response. I took a deep breath in, inhaling the scent of her and damn near choking on my own desire to get my hands on her. When her hand came up to rest on my chest, I reached out, curving my arm around her waist and pulling her closer to me.

"That's what I want to see," she said, voice going molten as she leaned up and in. Her lips moved, but I barely heard her words over the roaring of blood through my veins. Even my control could only take so much. "Women like it when you show a little initiative, Jonnie."

I swallowed hard as she pulled back. Initiative wasn't something I lacked but fuck, I was trying to be good and let her lead this. Clearly, there was a time and a place for that, and it wasn't right fucking now when all I could think about was having her under me. Decision made, I tightened my arm around her waist, making sure there was no space between us before gripping her chin. When her eyes widened, I didn't pause to overthink it, instead taking her lips with mine.

A soft puff of air brushed over my face, and I groaned when Regina's lips instantly opened for me. The taste of her lipstick was heady, but the flavor of her mouth was even better than before. I could taste the barest hint of wine as I brushed her tongue with mine, and I searched out that tang until all I could taste was her. The fabric of her dress was soft and slid under my hand as I turned us until I had her pressed against the door. I moved in, caging her so there was nowhere to go. I needed her right there, pinned against me until we melded into one.

"Fuck," Regina panted as she turned her face away to breathe. I felt my way across her cheek with my lips, tracing my way to her earlobe and taking it between my teeth. Her groan was more vibration than sound, and my hand slid from her chin to the back of her neck, gripping and angling her head up so I could taste her even deeper.

Slick sounds filled my ears as hands gripped my shoulders and back. I wanted her frantic, as frantic as my need was for her. I wanted my name to be the first word on her lips in the morning and the last that left her tongue at night. There was no going back.

Hands pushed on my tuxedo jacket, and I reluctantly loosened my clutch on her to unbutton it. I let the material fall down my arms before tossing it away, not caring where it landed. Regina leaned back before looking at me incredulously.

"Isn't that Gucci?"

"I don't fucking care," I growled out before cupping her cheeks and pulling her back in for another soul-rocking kiss. Clothes didn't fucking matter as long as I got her skin against mine. "I need you naked. Now."

With a strength I didn't know she had, Regina pushed me back until there were a few inches of space between us. We stood there, both panting like we had run a marathon. I knew the look in my eyes had to be wild. I felt out of control yet strangely composed. It was the type of focus I usually only got in the boardroom or at a business meeting when I knew I was going to get exactly what I wanted. Right now, all that focus was on stripping Regina down until there was nothing but need between us. My intentions must have been broadcast on my face because she held a hand up, stopping me from advancing.

"Jonnie, wait." I clenched my hands into fists as I fought the urge to move anyway. Her gaze lowered, glancing at one, then the other before she looked back up at me. "You cannot damage this dress."

I frowned, not understanding. "What?"

Regina huffed before gesturing at her dress. "This is Alexander McQueen."

"Well, I suggest you get it off now before I rip it from you stitch by stitch." The hitch in her breathing was a small, barely noticeable thing, yet it made my blood sing. My grin turned sharp, and I took a small step toward her, letting her know how serious I was. I knew exactly how much it cost, and I knew exactly how to get a replacement if need be. When she held her hand up again, I stopped. She turned around, giving me her back before looking over her shoulder.

"Unzip me." It wasn't a question, and I didn't treat it as such. I reached out, brushing my fingers over the nape of her neck. Her barely-there shiver pushed me to move lower, and I felt for the clasps and zippers holding the dress up. Each inch of new skin bared had my hunger growing until I could see the dip in her back. I didn't move away, instead stepping closer until I could dip my head down and suck a kiss where her neck and shoulder met.

My hands moved as if having a mind of their own, peeling the fabric down, and I kissed a trail down her back as I moved to kneel. When I reached her ass, I sucked in a breath at the small slip of fabric between full ass cheeks that were just begging to be fondled and loved. I kissed the small of her back, loving the hint of salt on her skin. The dress was easy enough to let fall to the ground, and I carefully helped her turn, not bothering to get up from where I was kneeling in front of her.

"You look good on your knees for me," Regina said, voice pitched low and deep. Her eyes seemed to glow as she watched me move the dress away, draping it over the door handle haphazardly. "Are you going to help me out of everything?" She shifted her hips up, showcasing the intricate lace front of her thong.

I hummed in response, sliding my hands up her right leg and lifting it until it rested over my shoulder. In this position, I could almost taste her on the back of my tongue, musky and heady. I turned my head, kissing her calf and following the line of her up. A hand cupped my cheek and forced me to pause and look up at her.

"Shoes first."

It was a short detour but one I happily took. I carefully undid the clasp of her strapped heel, mouthing the jut of her ankle. Worshipping her like this was easy. I would taste every part of her before the night was through.

When I had her feet bare, I turned my attention back to the small slip of fabric hiding her from my gaze. My head was abuzz with my need, and when Regina didn't stop me, I lifted her leg again, sliding the fabric down and teasing us both. When her hands shot out and gripped the back of my head, I went with the motion, willingly burying my nose in the dark curls in front of me. We hadn't even made it out of the foyer, but I was ready to fuck her against the door just to slake part of the monster banging on my skull, demanding to be set free on her.

"Hurry up," Regina said impatiently. Her fingers dug in, sending a thrill through me to feel her need so desperately. Everything about her had been controlled and careful up to this point, and I wanted to break that wall until she was as ravenously gone as me.

"Is there something you want?"

Regina's eyes narrowed, and she looked like she was ready to hit me, but I just grinned and held my ground. I wanted to hear her say exactly what she wanted from me. I needed to have those words in that voice painted in my memory for the nights when I went to bed alone and woke up even lonelier.

"Put your mouth to good use and fuck me with your tongue, otherwise I'll find someone else who will."

That had me surging upward, grabbing her wrists in my hands and pulling them up above her head. Lava, molten and unstoppable, pulsed through me as I glared down at her. "Oh, really? You'd find someone else who could make you come like I did? I fucking doubt that."

"You have a lot of ego to think I haven't already had someone make me come hard." Her voice was like a whip digging down to the bone, and I surged against it. She wanted to push me, and I knew it, but I wanted to be pushed. I wanted to let this fire out and scorch us both on the flames.

"Who would you look for, hmm? Liam?" I spit his name out with a grimace. "You think that pretty boy could make you scream in anything but frustration?"

I felt her fight against my hold, but I pressed harder, keeping her hands trapped above her against the door. She gave me a wild grin of her own as she leaned her head forward, moving our faces closer. "And if I did? What are you going to do? Offer a ring to your ex Melania and go have a perfectly respectable, boring life?"

I wasn't sure where the fuck that was coming from, but I didn't care. All I knew was I needed to show her she was mine, no one else's. Regina had clawed her way under my skin ten years ago, and if anything was proven the past few weeks, it was that she had never left. Getting over her was not an option. Before I could pause to think, I whirled Regina around until I was pressed tightly against her back. I transferred her wrists to one hand before using the other to unzip my pants and push them down.

Regina wasn't still against me, pushing her ass out and nearly making my eyes cross at the friction. Scraping sounds had me grinning fiercely as her nails clawed against the door. "Hurry up and fuck me, you asshole." Her words were like oxygen, fanning the flames of my lust higher. "I hate you so fucking much."

I chuckled darkly into the shell of her ear as I closed a hand around my dick, sliding it up and down the globes of her ass before I took a step back and forced her to follow. Her back arched, making me wish I had a camera to capture the slope of it and the way the faint light from the living room played with the shadows on her skin.

"No, you don't hate me," I whispered heatedly. "You wanted me the moment we saw each other. But it's okay. I wanted you to. You're mine, Regina. I'll kill anyone else who tries to touch you like this."

She chuckled, glancing over her shoulder. "That's the Jonnie I knew was there. Nice doesn't suit you."

I dug my teeth into my lip as I stroked my dick over the crack of her ass and down to where she was hot and slick, just waiting to be taken. She was right about one thing. Nice wasn't me, nor was I passive. Only she could draw this side out of me, and I liked it too much to seal it away again. This relationship might have started out with a contract, but I wouldn't rest until she was painted on the inside with nothing but thoughts of me.

The first push in was like coming home and falling apart all at once. Regina dropped her head, letting out a wild sound, and I had to grip her hip to keep from slamming us both against the door as I sheathed myself fully. "So fucking wet, baby. No one else gets you wet like this, do they?"

When she didn't answer, I lifted my hand from her hip, taking hold of her chin once again and angling her head so I could mouth kisses against her cheek. She looked defiant, a queen holding out until the last moment, and it made me smirk. I didn't want to break her. I wanted to fuse us together into something so much more.

"Answer me," I hissed, pressing my mouth against her cheek. Her lips parted as I got closer to them but instead of kissing, I slid my hips back before lunging forward inside of her. The soft cry of pleasure falling from that mouth was too enticing to ignore, and I leaned in, taking her lips with my own to taste the flavor of her pleasure.

We moved together, me thrusting slow but deep, enjoying the little hop off her toes as I got balls-deep inside of her. Slick sounds accompanied our grunts and moans of pleasure, and I let go of Regina's wrists in favor of propping myself against the door. One of her hands did the same while the other reached back, taking hold of my ass and demanding more. I was helpless to do anything but oblige.

"Fuck," she slurred out, head falling back against my shoulder. I took advantage, sucking a mark into the silky skin of her neck. My hand, now free, immediately found the hard jut of her nipples, plucking them like strings as I enjoyed the notes that fell from her parted lips. When her muscles clenched, I knew she was close. "Right there. Fuck, harder, goddamnit."

I concentrated on that spot, fucking up harder, wanting to see her fall apart. When I felt her nails dig into my ass, I groaned and held on tight as her body pulsed. Regina fell forward against the door as she jerked, and I followed, pressing deep into her. When she sighed, movements coming to a stop, I slid my hand up, curling it around her throat. My hips flexed, dick still hard and ready to show her all the ways it could pleasure her. Once would never be enough.

"I hope you don't think I'm done with you," I whispered over the shell of her ear. "We have all night."

Chapter Twenty

Regina

Everything was sore, and I shifted in my chair as I stared at the Excel sheet in front of me. It made sense, but I would much rather be doing something else than reading them. It was a necessary evil for the meeting I was supposed to have later, but really, all I wanted was a nice deep tub with some fragrant water to rest my aching body, regardless of where the aches came from. Something had clearly changed between Jonathan and me.

Never mind the fact that my libido had decided to kick itself into fucking overdrive. It was like once I gave myself permission to fuck him, it decided it was time to go for broke. It had been a week since the gala, and every night ended with me in his arms or my hand around his throat as I rode him for filth. And fuck, was it good. I'd known sex was a great workout, but the boost to my mood was new. Had I known good sex would have that effect, I might not have abstained as much as I had in the past.

My cell ringing caught me off guard, but when I checked the time, I realized more time had passed than I thought. "This is Regina."

"Regina. It's Anthony from Carson Realty."

His voice was pleasant, though I couldn't remember exactly what he looked like. We had met at the gala thanks to Jonathan's influence and now I needed to get things going. I had scouted a couple of locations I knew they had on their real estate roster, and I wanted to get the jump on the two I found that looked the most promising. "I know we were going to meet at four, but a few things have come up."

I tightened my grip on the phone. Surely he wasn't cancelling on me already? "Oh, no. Did you need to reschedule?"

"Well, I was hoping you might have some time earlier to meet with us at the Five Points location. Say around one?"

I glanced at the clock. That was less than two hours from now, but for this deal, I would make it work. "That works perfectly for me, actually. I have some other properties I planned on reviewing out that way around the same time."

"Perfect," Anthony said. We exchanged a few more sentences before ending the call, and I tried not to let the abrupt change throw off my review of the numbers in front of me. Everything was still so tentative that whenever unexpected changes occurred, I was never sure how to handle them.

I shook my head and regrouped. Devolving into spiraling thoughts wasn't the way to get through this. I couldn't show any hesitancy when it came to these things, especially not with me, for all intents and purposes, being a newcomer on the business scene. I doubted most people even remembered my last name, and it wouldn't do me any favors regardless. Light glinting caught my attention, and I looked down at the ring on my finger.

I could begrudgingly agree that Jonathan had picked out the perfect ring. Never had I imagined one on my finger, but now that it was, I could admit it suited my style. It wasn't small, but it also wasn't some overly gaudy thing that looked like we were trying too hard. When I had sent the news of the engagement to my parents, neither of them had said much, though I knew they would once it completely sank in. Especially my dad. For now, I would enjoy the fact that I hadn't gotten any angry phone calls just yet.

Soon enough, I found myself in the car on my way to meet Anthony. Traffic was as terrible as always, but I made sure to take note of the parking in the area. The area was already built up as it was, so I knew there was an audience for the place. Still, I needed to get an idea of the locals to see just how to tap into that market successfully. When I parked, two men walked toward me, and I clenched my hand around my purse. When they reached me, the shorter man reached a hand out, and I vaguely remembered him from the gala.

"Anthony. It's good to meet you again," he said with a toothy smile. His dirty blonde hair was perfectly styled and the suit he had one probably cost more than my car. Still, he seemed sincere in his greeting, so I returned his smile and shook his hand. He gestured to his companion, and I ran my gaze over him as well. He wasn't as put together as Anthony, but with his slicked back brown hair and lightly tanned babyface, he was probably harmless. "This is Clarence. He's our newest intern and learning the ropes, so I thought this would be a good chance for him to get an idea of the business."

I was a little annoyed that I would have an audience, but I nodded anyway and shook Clarence's hand as well. Being rude wouldn't do me any favors, so I fixed a smile on my face and followed the men into the building.

The space was industrial, with tall ceilings and ductwork that lent to the feel. I listened to Anthony talk and made plans in my head for what the space could potentially be. I had seen some of my dad's plans for getting back into the restaurant scene, so I'd decided to use them with a more modern flair. It would fit the space and give a new vibe to a well-loved area.

Anthony continued talking as we viewed the property, sharing a little history of the space while also giving me insight into the area. I appreciated his candor as I would need that to make the best choice possible. When we were back at the front of the building, I couldn't stop myself from smiling at the possibilities spread before me in this space.

"This place looks amazing, Anthony," I said, bringing the conversation back. "I can definitely see this working for what I have envisioned."

He nodded with a grin. "Wonderful. And Jonathan? Will he need to come see the space as well before you all make a decision?"

"He isn't involved in this project." The mood changed, and Anthony's smile seemed to dim for a moment. "Is that going to be a problem?"

He held his hands open before tilting his head. "To be quite frank, it does present a slight dilemma for us. We were hoping this would be a joint venture with Dummond—"

"I am quite capable of handling my business solo," I said, trying to keep my voice calm as a hot core of anger welled up within me. What the hell was this guy trying to pull? Was Jonathan behind this? No, it didn't seem like his style, and he knew how much I wanted him to stay out of my business. "Is the other space close?"

Anthony paused, and I had to clench my fists to keep from lunging at him to shake him. If he was just going to waste my time, I was going to leave.

I was lying when I said I had other stops for the day, but he didn't need to know that. I needed him to see this as a deal too valuable to lose. I reached deep into the well of confidence that had served me on more than one occasion. If he wanted to start with the bullshit, I would match him for it step by step.

I stood up taller, raising my head slightly as if looking down at him. Pushing me around was not something I would entertain regardless of who he might know. "I have a busy day planned with other locations to review, so we can either hurry this along or I will take my time elsewhere."

Anthony and Clarence exchanged looks before Anthony pulled out his phone. I smirked until I saw him dial a number instead of pull up directions. *Who the fuck could he possibly be calling?* I did drop my façade. If he wanted to escalate, I was ready.

When Jonathan's voice came over the line, I almost slapped the damn phone from Anthony's hands.

"Anthony."

"Mr. Dummond. It's good to speak with you. I have a Ms. Regina here looking at our Five Points property for a potential restaurant investment."

Jonathan was quiet for a moment, and I clenched my jaw to stop a scream from working its way from my mouth. Who the fuck did this man think he was? I was ready to let loose my frustration on him until I heard Jonathan speak again.

"And that has what to do with me?" His voice sounded bored, but I could hear the warning under that even tone. It gave me pause. "Her business is her own."

Anthony glanced at me before looking back at the phone. "Yes, however, this represents a substantial—"

"Are you doubting my fiancée's understanding of what she wants?" His tone turned sharp, and I couldn't help the thrill that went through me as I watched Anthony stammer out a response. "I fully support her vision for her work and don't need to be involved to know it will be successful. I suggest you listen to her instead of attempting to garner goodwill with me."

Even Clarence looked chastised, and I shifted, crossing my arms as I watched them squirm. While I wanted to beat the brakes off this fool for calling Jonathan in the first place, the fact that this was the result was refreshing. Hopefully, they would talk, and word would spread. I hated that I even needed an in to get shit done, but if me watching people choke on their bullshit was going to be the result, I wouldn't mind pulling the Jonathan card more often.

He was a resource after all, and if he wanted to be used, I would squeeze out every drop.

I fixed a less smug smile on my face when Anthony hung up the phone with shaking hands. His smile was watery, and I almost snorted at how pathetic he seemed now that the person he was attempting to suck up to had handed him his ass.

"You said you were curious about the second location?"

As much as I wanted to tell him to fuck off, the locations truly were perfect for my plans. Still, I couldn't help but fuck with him a bit, drawing out the silence as I stared him down. Finally, I nodded sharply.

"Lead the way."

~*~*~

The day ended better than it had begun, and I was all smiles when I pulled into the garage at Jonathan's condo. I knew he was already in. He'd been strangely eager about seeing me for the evening, which was weird given we'd been in one another's space consistently for the entire week. There were still some unspoken words that needed to be had, particularly regarding the little discussion I overheard in the gala bathroom. Still, I wasn't sure if I was ready to handle a conversation that I couldn't explain away as being just about business.

I wasn't naïve. I knew what jealousy felt like, and I was fucking jealous. Possessively so. Jonathan has practically prostrated himself in front of me in order to get me to forgive him. That had to mean something.

"And why do I care so fucking much?" I muttered to myself as I climbed out of the car. I slammed it shut and paused. I prided myself on understanding exactly where my head was at all times. I didn't do miscommunication.

Thoughts ran through my mind as I made my way into the building. When the door opened before I could grab the handle, I jerked to a stop and looked up. I barely moved in time before another woman came out. I shifted over, giving her space to move, but when she looked up at me, her eyes widened.

I froze. The woman looked a few years older than me, but although there was a small tickle at the back of my mind, I didn't think I knew her. She glanced behind her, but there was no one there. Worry slowly filled me.

"Are you okay?" I asked, not sure why she looked so shifty. "Are you looking for someone?"

She looked back at me before shaking her head. "No. I'm sorry. I shouldn't have—" She cut herself off abruptly before pushing past me and rushing into the garage. Before she turned the corner, she paused and peeked at me over her shoulder, but when she saw I was still standing there, she hurried on, disappearing from view.

"What the fuck was that all about?" I stood there for a moment longer, not sure if I should run after the woman or call someone to make sure she wasn't casing the place. The sound of a car honking shook me from my musing, and I made my way into the building as planned.

During the elevator ride up to Jonathan's penthouse, I tried to think if I had ever seen the woman before. I didn't remember her at the gala, and I hadn't been in town long enough to really know people unless they were introduced to me by Christa or Jonathan.

I pushed the other woman from my mind when the elevator doors opened, and I stepped out. The door to the penthouse was unlocked, and when I entered, the scent of tomato sauce filled the air.

"Are you actually cooking? I thought you hired out all those mundane tasks like doing laundry and feeding yourself," I said as I walked through the foyer and into the open living room. Jonathan was at the stove, and he turned to look at me with a smile.

"Sometimes I like to change things up a little," he replied.

I raised an eyebrow. "Should I be worried about being poisoned?" He chuckled but I still cast a dubious look at the pot.

"I don't think so," he said. When he saw my expression, he shook his head before gesturing to the already set dining table. "It's just spaghetti. Take a seat and I'll bring the plates over."

I nodded. If there was ever a time when I was going to do what someone said, it would be when it came to food. Especially food that I didn't have to cook myself. I sat down in the spot I had unofficially claimed for myself. Beside Jonathan's setting was a folder. I frowned when I looked at it.

"Are you trying to get me to sign more paperwork?"

"What?"

When he walked over to the table with two plates in his hands, I gestured at the folder. He set the plates down before taking a seat beside me.

"Oh. No. I think Kevin dropped this off in my mailbox, so I was going to look over it."

I nodded before looking down at the heaping helping of ravioli. "Trying to fatten me up?"

Jonathan smiled sharply as he dragged his gaze over me. "Not trying to. But you're usually amenable to sex when you have a full belly."

I slapped his hand, though I didn't deny it. Food sex wasn't a thing for me, but good sex *after* good food absolutely was.

"Well, keep playing your cards right and maybe I'll let you stuff me full of something other than just pasta."

His eyes darkened, but he said nothing as he picked up his fork and started eating. I did the same, eyes nearly rolling back in my head when the flavor of tomatoes and ricotta hit my tongue. Good dick and good food. I might have to marry this fool for real. It wasn't as unwelcome a thought as it had been weeks ago. Jonathan's presence had been unobtrusive enough to grow on me, especially after hearing him put Anthony in his place this afternoon.

"Oh, I forgot," I said after finishing another bite of cheese-filled heaven. "I want to thank you for what you said today. To Anthony."

Jonathan paused, fork in the air as he looked at me. His eyes had widened, and I rolled my own in response. I didn't know why he seemed so surprised. I knew how to be grateful when the situation called for it. Just because I had never been grateful to him before didn't mean I would take things for granted.

"I didn't want to overstep, but when he made the insinuation I had to sign off on something that had to do with you and not me—"

"I know," I replied, cutting him off. "I appreciated it. It was actually quite sexy."

"Oh?"

I nodded slowly before standing and leaning over toward him. This close, I could see when his pupils dilated and felt a soft puff of air as he breathed. Somehow, every time we were close like this, I found myself almost drowning in my own desire. Jonathan's lips were wet from where he'd licked them earlier, and I leaned closer, narrowing my eyes when his tongue came out to swipe that same spot again. When my hand landed on top of the folder, it jolted me out of the moment, and instead of taking his lips, I let my mouth close around his still-raised fork.

"Mmm," I hummed as I moved back to my seat. "You really are quite good at this cooking thing."

Jonathan was still sat frozen as his gaze tracked me. When I went back to my own plate, his eyes narrowed, and I only had a moment to brace myself before my chair was pulled out and I was lifted up by strong arms wrapped around my waist.

"You are a fucking tease," he growled out, voice rough with arousal. It sent shivers running through me, but I grinned. I loved the wildness of him, and as hungry as I was for food, I wanted him even more.

"A tease doesn't usually follow through," I whispered against his mouth before dipping in for a kiss. His usual taste was slightly covered by tomato, but it was still undeniably him. I licked deeper, pushing him back slightly, but the sound of glass falling over pulled me out of the mood we had both fallen into. Jonathan turned to grab the glass of wine that was knocked over, but when I went for the napkin, the folder fell over, its contents spilling onto the floor.

Jonathan and I looked at one another for a moment before breaking out into soft laughter. "Maybe we should finish dinner before trying to skip to dessert." I chuckled and leaned down to grab the papers while he cleaned up the mess on the table.

Most of the papers had random numbers on them that wouldn't make sense unless I knew the context, but I couldn't care less. I wasn't interested in getting into Jonathan's business any more than I was in him being involved with mine. I opened the folder to shove the papers back in when a small slip caught my attention. It was a picture, clearly taken at some distance, but it wasn't the distance that surprised me. It was the woman in it.

The woman I had run into when I walked into the building.

I leaned back on my heels as I stared at the photo. She was younger there, and with the lack of age came more familiarity. I did know her. Or *of* her, rather. I had seen her before.

"Jonathan," I started before standing. He had walked into the kitchen, carting several napkins stained red with spilled wine. He tossed them in the sink before looking back at me, expression open and amused. I lifted the photo. "Who is this woman?"

He cocked his head to the side before looking down at it.

"That's what I'm trying to figure out." He turned on the water in the sink, rinsing his hands. "I've been running an audit on the company, and there's a subsidiary we aren't quite sure what to make of. I had an employee do some deep dives, and it came back to her, whoever she is."

I looked back at the photo, trying to understand. It wasn't a mistake, though. I knew I had seen this woman even prior to tonight. I narrowed my eyes and tried to think. I didn't have a name to go with the face, but suddenly, a memory popped into my head.

"I think I know her." When Jonathan's eyes widened, I quickly clarified. "Well, not know her, but I've seen her before."

Jonathan dried his hands haphazardly before striding back to my side. "Where? What's her name?"

I shook my head. "I don't know her name, but I saw her tonight when I was coming into your building." I was sure of it. It was the same woman. "And I saw her before then too. With your dad."

Chapter Twenty-One

Jonathan

The Atlanta skyline had a chokehold on my gaze but not my thoughts. Those were moving at a breakneck pace as I tried to sort through what little information I had on me now. The revelation that the woman who Kevin had found as the owner of the nonexistent Patterson Construction had not only been sighted in my building but also years ago with my father had my head spinning for the past few days. It hadn't made any sense to me. We didn't even have a name for her, and while Regina could recall seeing her a couple times, that was all she had.

I needed to understand. Who the hell was this woman and why was she involved in a company under the Dummond umbrella? Why was there a barren field where construction should be? What the fuck was my father hiding?

A knock on the door broke through my thoughts, and I called out for the person to enter. The door opened, revealing Jameson. He walked in, frown set on his face, before falling into the chair across from my desk. He didn't look any happier than I was.

"Where's mom?"

He shook his head. "She refused to come. Said she didn't have any desire to walk down memory fucking lane." He narrowed his eyes. "What the hell is going on, Jonnie?"

"I wish I fucking knew," I said with a huff as I sat back in my chair. When another knock came, I schooled my expression and gave Jameson a pointed look. He sat up, expression closing off in that way that always reminded me of our childhood. I hated that he even knew how to do that, but I could admit it came in handy in situations like now when we needed to do what was necessary to get answers.

When Braselton walked through the doorway, I wanted to wipe the smug expression off his face with my fist. I wondered if he knew what this was all about or if he really was foolish enough to think I actually wanted to see him. I had been biding my time until I was ready to send him out on his ass, and we were quickly approaching that glorious moment.

"Jonathan, I was wondering when I would have a moment to speak with you," Braselton said. He spared a glance at Jameson, and I saw his smile twitch slightly. That little tell was enough to propel me forward. I stood up and walked around the desk.

"Wonderful," I replied with false cheer. I needed to keep him off guard before I pressed him. It wouldn't do to get him on the defensive already. I needed him to think I was on his side before I crushed his ass beneath my heel. "Jameson and I were looking over some things with the most recent audit, and when we had questions, we knew you were the one to reach out to."

That had him preening, and I saw Jameson's lip quirk up. He knew exactly what I was playing at. We'd perfected this routine when we were younger and wanted to pump people for information we shouldn't have in the first place.

"Always glad to be of help," Braselton said as he walked over and sat in the chair beside Jameson. "Your father always said I helped him when it came to figuring out the next move to make."

I nodded before leaning back to perch on the edge of my desk. "You've mentioned that a couple of times. I know he had a lot of faith in your work here."

Braselton sat up straighter, puffing his chest out like he was in a dick-measuring contest. It was useless posturing, but I let him have it. "He absolutely did. We did a lot of great work together, your father and I, God rest his soul."

I wanted to snort at the idea of God and my father in the same sentence. If anything, he was probably somewhere down below giving the Devil a run for his money. Jameson spoke up, continuing the conversation.

"I remember him mentioning the trips you all used to take down to Savannah. My fiancée has expressed some interest in us moving down there and I was talking to Jonathan about taking up some of the work in that location." Braselton's expression didn't change, but that didn't mean anything just yet. I watched him carefully as Jameson continued spinning his story. McKenzie had zero desire to leave the city, but Braselton didn't need to know that. All we needed from him was a single slip-up—a string we could follow to the woman in the photo.

A name, damn it. All I needed was a goddamn name.

"I think, for safety's sake, you and McKenzie should probably be somewhat outside the city. You would really only need to go into the office a couple times a week as is," I said, drawing Braselton's attention. I could feel his eyes on me, but I kept my own gaze on Jameson as if we were just shooting the shit and not spinning a story. "Especially once you start thinking of children. What do you think?"

When I looked back at him, Braselton almost snapped to attention, head moving up and down like a bobble toy.

"Yes, I agree. Savannah can be so unsafe for young women."

"Wait," Jameson said, slapping his hands together as if he had just had a profound idea. It made me want to snicker. Acting was not his forte, but Braselton seemed somehow enraptured, no doubt by the idea that we were trusting him with some information—inviting him into the fold. "Didn't father build some luxury residential neighborhood down in…what's the place called? Glasgow?"

Braselton frowned. "There's no development in—" He abruptly stopped talking, eyes widening when Jameson and I both looked at him in faux confusion. "I mean, Glasgow is too far from Savannah."

"What were you going to say?" I asked, pushing the fake confusion angle. I turned to pick up the file on my desk and opened it. "I had Kevin check. Father built that area nine or ten years ago. You and McKenzie should probably go check it out first, though."

From the corner of my eye, I could see Braselton twist his hands together. He was starting to sweat, but I wanted to push him farther. I needed him to spill open before I could cut him loose.

Jameson nodded. "Why don't you and Regina come with us? I know you mentioned that woman was following her. It would probably be good for her to get out of town for a bit."

"What woman?" Braselton asked. I looked over at him with what I hoped was an unassuming smile.

"There was a woman following Regina for a moment." I picked up the picture that had started this whole thing and handed it to him. Braselton looked confused until the moment he saw the image. His face drained of color, and I knew then he knew exactly who the woman was. When he looked up at me, I was sure I had him. "I had to call security, and I'm thinking of providing Regina with extra protection as well until this woman is found."

"That's so scary," Jameson piped up, shaking his head with a sorrowful expression that almost made me lose it completely. "Whoever she is working with needs to be investigated. I could probably reach out to—"

"That won't be necessary."

We both turned to look at Braselton. He was still looking down at the photo, his hand shaking slightly. I reached out, putting my finger on the woman's face. "Do you know who this woman is?"

He looked up at me before nodding slowly. When I narrowed my eyes, he was quick to attempt to be reassuring. "But I know she means Regina no harm."

"How do you know that?" Jameson asked. "Are you working with this woman?"

"No!" Braselton said explosively. He stood up from his chair and tossed the picture onto my desk before walking over to the windows. When Jameson made a move to stand, I stuck my hand out, stopping him. I took a step forward, my eyes trained on Braselton's back.

"Michael," I called out, keeping my voice even. He didn't turn to look at me, but his shoulders moved up and down in response. "Who is this woman?"

He was quiet for a moment longer before turning to face me. "She is—was—your father's mistress."

I wasn't shocked that father had a mistress. It was well-known gossip, though most were discreet with their whispers. What I didn't understand was why she was here now. I didn't remember seeing her at the funeral, though I had been preoccupied.

"Why is she sneaking around now?" I asked.

"I don't know."

"You can't honestly expect us to believe that," Jameson insisted, standing up from his chair. "You knew enough who she was."

Braselton held up his hands. "I didn't know all the details, just that she and your father had a relationship. He gifted her the property down in Glasgow with the understanding that they were through and had me hide it in one of our subsidiaries."

I nodded. It sounded like something that bastard would do. "That doesn't explain why money is still being funneled into the project, given that it doesn't exist." When Braselton bit his lip, I almost rushed at him. My aborted motion seemed to startle him into talking again.

"Your father didn't tell me everything," he said, taking a step back until his back was at the window. "But he gave me a code to a safe at your house. He told me to keep quiet about it."

Jameson and I exchanged looks. It wasn't a surprise he would store shit in a house we all tried to stay away from. That mother didn't know about it was. "Where in the house is the safe?"

"And what is the fucking code for it?" I growled out. Jameson lifted a hand to grip my shoulder, and it was the only thing keeping me grounded. It had been one fucking thing after another, and I was tired of being the last one to know shit.

I was supposed to be the heir taking on the running of this company, yet I was still finding out new shit that made my life difficult six months after burying the bastard whose DNA I happened to inherit. I was tired of this shit. "The code, Michael."

He dropped his head down, the fight gone from his frame, and I felt a sick sense of glee that I was going to get exactly what I wanted.

"Five-four-seven-one," he said finally, voice quiet but not soft enough for me to not hear him.

"If you're lying to us—"

"I'm not," he said quickly, lifting his head. "I promise. There's nothing left to protect. Your dad is gone, and I'm tired of keeping his fucking secrets. He promised me a new position and yet here I am, still playing second fiddle to a bunch of—"

"Choose your words wisely," Jameson growled out. His hand gripped my shoulder tightly, but now I wondered who was really being held back. Braselton seemed to get the hint.

"I will be submitting my resignation by the end of the day."

I glared at him for a moment before nodding sharply. "Fine. I expect you to leave all evidence of anything else you helped our father cover up over the years. If I have to come looking for you…" I let my voice trail off. In truth, I wouldn't have to do anything. Once Jennifer heard what was going on, she would be on his trail in no time to ensure he complied.

"Of course." He skirted around the chairs, doing his best to keep a wide berth. Jameson and I watched him, but beyond that, we didn't move. When he reached the door, he threw it open, moving quickly before disappearing from sight. It was only when the sound of his footsteps faded away that I allowed myself to relax. I knew we had a lot more to uncover, and I was not looking forward to the fallout.

~*~*~

"This has to be a mistake."

I sighed before looking up at Jalissa. As soon as Braselton left, Jameson had immediately gone into the group chat and called a house meeting.

Getting everyone to show up without spilling the beans via text had been difficult, but not as fucked up as having to explain to them what was discovered. I was only happy that our mother seemed to be out again instead of witnessing the shit show of opening the safe and pulling out secrets none of us had even the faintest inkling of.

A hidden fucking will.

Folders of documents none of us had even known existed. Papers were spread out on the dining table between us as we took turns mining for bullshit. Bank accounts. Secret properties. It shouldn't have been so surprising, yet all I could do was sigh when a new piece of information was uncovered.

"This shit goes back decades," Jennifer said, holding up a document that I knew was a contract for another property that didn't exist. We had found ten of those so far, mostly in Georgia but a couple in other states. "How the hell did we not know any of this existed?"

"Because the old man was a lying fuck," Jameson said, tossing another paper onto the ongoing pile of shit. He leaned back with a groan and threw an arm over his face. I knew exactly how he was feeling, but I turned my attention back to the forms in my hand. Jerome was grumbling, and every other word from Jalissa was only four letters long, but it was the next page in the stack in front of me that caught my full attention.

"What the fuck is this?"

My voice was loud enough to be heard by all of them, and I instantly felt four sets of eyes on me. I quickly read through, a sickening feeling growing in my gut. Rage, pure and molten, welled up in me at what was on the page. My hands shook as I clenched my fingers, damn near ripping the thing in half just to get it away from me. When Jameson reached over to snatch it away, I didn't even fight him.

He was quiet for a moment before a small curse left his mouth. I pushed back from the table, my chair scraping loudly on the floor. I needed to hit something. I needed the comforting feeling of something solid meeting my knuckles to keep me from digging the fucker up and setting him on fire.

"What is it?" Jerome asked. Blood was pumping through my ears so quickly it damn near made it hard to hear. I walked over to the wall and, without bothering to think about it, slammed my fist against it.

"Father…has another kid."

Hearing Jameson say it made it more real. But it was fucking impossible. We would have known that he had an entire fucking family besides us. Mother at least would have had an idea. How the hell could he have possibly hidden that for years without anyone talking about it?

"That's not…" I turned and leaned my head back against the wall, hoping that the coolness would calm me. Jennifer was staring at me, expression open for once. The disbelief was clear and mirrored in Jalissa. "That's not all it—" I couldn't even finish my damn sentence without feeling a surge of rage.

"Fuck," Jerome said as he leaned back in his chair as well. "He really was a bastard."

I snorted, though there was no humor in the sound. Insurance. That's what he'd bought himself. "It gets better," I gritted out between clenched teeth. "Keep fucking reading."

Jameson sighed loudly before he continued. "It looks like there's an extra clause in the will that…" He trailed off, turning to look at me. I pushed off the wall and walked back to the table.

"That cancels out all of your inheritances in the event I don't marry before this kid's eighteenth birthday."

"What the fuck!"

"Can he do that?" Jalissa asked, looking between all of us. "He's dead now. Can he…is that really enforceable?"

Jerome shrugged, looking sick at the implication. "I doubt the old man would have half-assed this. Not with the way he was." He gestured to Jameson. "When is the kid's birthday?"

Jameson kept reading. When he turned the page and paused, I think we all held our collective breaths. "Fuck, man. I don't think—"

"Just fucking say it," I bit out. When he looked at me, I shrugged. There wasn't a damn thing we could do about this shit now. "How long have we got?"

He sighed again before speaking. "Less than a month."

"There's no way he can get married in a month!" Jalissa exclaimed. "That's not enough time to plan anything, and you don't even want to—"

"It's fine." Her mouth closed with a click. The room grew silent, but I pretty much knew what they were thinking. I turned to Jameson. "You're still ordained, right?"

Jameson's eyes widened. "I mean, yeah, but you can't expect me to just be okay marrying you off for our inheritance."

I wasn't okay with it, but I didn't see a choice. I was the oldest. Protecting my siblings was what I did, even if the person I was protecting them from was dead. It wasn't like I never planned on marriage. The ring on Regina's finger was proof of that. But I hadn't wanted my hand forced when it came to it. This was father's way of getting in one last 'fuck you' from the grave, and if it lost me Regina again, I really would dig his ass up for a bonfire.

Chapter Twenty-Two

Regina

I was just stepping out of the shower when I heard the doorbell ring. With a frown, I wrapped a towel around myself and walked out of the bathroom. I wasn't expecting company tonight. It was one of the few nights when Jonathan was usually busy with his family. I had been around them a couple of times, mostly for dinner, but I hadn't yet spent time with them all since the gala. I figured they were still getting used to me like I was. It was strange to have to navigate four or five different conversations at a time. Life even with Casey around wasn't usually like that. Still, I couldn't deny it was sort of fun to watch Jonathan's siblings take the piss out of him the way only siblings could. It humanized him and made him seem less like his dad.

I grabbed a pair of sweats and tossed them on, forgoing underwear to see who the hell was at my damn door this late at night. When I looked through the peephole, I was shocked to see Liam standing there. I paused for a moment before unlocking the door and opening it.

"Liam. What are you doing here?"

He looked sober and put-together, but there was still an edge in the air, and I kept my door open only a crack. I had a doorbell camera, as did several of my hallway neighbors, but I was still wary. We had hardly spoken in weeks, and even at the gala, he'd barely acted like I existed.

"I need to talk to you about something."

"Okay," I said, not sure of what to make of his tone. "Talk."

He glanced over my head. "You aren't going to invite me inside?"

"No." My answer was simple and straightforward. I didn't trust him like that to let him have free rein of my space. "I was getting ready for bed."

He nodded. "Right, well, I just wanted to talk about how things went down between us."

Really? I thought to myself. "Liam, there was no us. We had the beginnings of a business arrangement and that's it."

He frowned. "Are you serious right now? We had nothing?"

I gave him a look. "Anything we could have had, you put the brakes on, so I'm not sure what you want me to say."

"Say you'll give me another chance."

"No. I'm with someone now."

He leaned forward into my space and narrowed his eyes. "You mean Dummond? He wouldn't even know what to do with it."

"And you do?" I scoffed. "You had your chance and you fumbled. I've moved on, and so should you. I'm sure there are plenty of women who would be more than happy to hang on your arm, but I'm not one of them." I moved to close the door, but his hand shot out, grabbing my arm. I tried to jerk away, glaring at him when his fingers dug harder into my skin.

"Liam, let me go."

"Not until you listen to me," he insisted. "Dummond is no good for you. I know things about him—"

I tried pulling away again, tendrils of panic starting to spread through me. I knew people were home and would probably hear me if I yelled, but I wasn't trying to become part of the latest gossip in the building.

"Liam, stop it. You're hurting me."

"You don't understand. Jonathan is not—"

Another hand shot out, grabbing Liam by the back of the neck and jerking him away from me. The sudden release of my arm had me falling slightly forward until I landed on a firm, familiar chest.

"She told you to let go." Jonathan's voice was like thunder rumbling out from somewhere deep within and forcing you to take notice.

Liam stared up at us from his sprawled position, but whatever element of surprise Jonathan had didn't last long. Liam stood, hands clenched into fists at his sides.

"This doesn't concern you, Dummond."

"If it concerns my future wife, it concerns me."

That had my heart pounding faster, and I couldn't help but glance up at Jonathan. I didn't know why he was here, but I couldn't deny I was grateful. The way he said "future wife" had me fighting off a giddy smile. I must be in shock to find that comforting, but I did. Whatever was happening here, I was fully on board for.

Liam shifted, and I wondered what his plan was a half-second before he lunged forward. I didn't know what he was expecting, but it probably wasn't to have his ass handed to him and end up back on the floor with blood dripping from his nose. Jonathan stood in front of me, muscles tight and stance screaming out he was not to be fucked with. I felt my mouth go dry. This couldn't be the same man who groaned in pleasure when I had my hand around his throat, yet it was. Jonathan was a man of layers, many of which I wanted to dig into and peel apart.

"Try that again and I'll do more than just rough up that pretty face of yours," Jonathan rumbled out. When one of the doors across the hall opened a crack, I knew it was time to wrap this up. I reached out and took Jonathan's hand.

"Liam, go home," I said, keeping my voice even and calm to not antagonize him. I didn't bother telling him what would happen if he didn't. I was pretty sure he got the idea. Plus, all my attention was on Jonathan and figuring out the best way to utilize that controlled strength.

I pulled him by the hand, walking us back until I could close the door and block out everything that wasn't us. Jonathan's muscles were still tense as I led him over to the couch. I pushed him down, sitting beside him and wondering how the hell this was my life.

"What are you doing here?" I asked after a few minutes of us sitting quietly. "Did you know Liam was coming over here? You could have warned me not to answer my damn door."

Jonathan shook his head. "I had no idea. If I had, I would have bashed his fucking head in before he reached your floor."

Not that the threat of violence wasn't sexy, but it was so out of character for Jonathan that it worried me. "What is going on? You're acting really—"

"Marry me."

I frowned at being interrupted. "You already asked me once. I'm wearing your ring."

He turned to look at me before gathering my hands in his. "No, not in six months or a year. Marry me now. This week."

I widened my eyes, wondering if he'd hit his head on the way over. "Jonathan, what are you talking about? We can't get married this week. We don't even like—"

"I've been in love with you since I was nineteen." His words had me slack-jawed with shock. This was not what I was expecting tonight at all. "I should have told you that then, and I regretted it every day after you left."

His words had my heart beating a furious beat. But as much as a part of me wanted to give in and scream out yes for reasons more than just the way it would help my business, I was still hesitant. Something wasn't right.

"Did you do this with your last fiancée? Just come at her with demands to marry within a week?" As much as I tried to keep my voice even, I couldn't help but almost spit out the word "fiancée."

I'd told myself it was no big deal. I had obviously known that Jonathan had been engaged before but hearing it from that woman's mouth had my jealousy poking its head out and making itself known.

Jonathan frowned. "My last fiancée?"

"Melania."

His expression didn't change at hearing her name. "I only asked her to marry me to fulfill what I thought was my duty to my name." He leaned towards me. "But then I realized I would rather be a disappointment than marry someone I didn't even like, let alone love."

Hope sprung anew in my chest, and I hated to have to tamp it down, but I was still unconvinced. Jonathan had seemed more than content to let this thing between us unfurl at its own pace. Tonight was coming completely out of left field, and I didn't like it.

"We both agreed to a long engagement," I reminded him. "And I need to make sure I'm not going to be surprised by any other former fiancées at these events."

Jonathan nodded. "I'll tell you everything."

"Good," I said curtly, nodding once. "Then you can start by telling me why you suddenly want to rush us into marriage."

"Regina—"

"No," I said, cutting him off this time. "Something must have happened. Tell me what's going on or I'll take this ring off and fly back to London tomorrow."

For a moment, Jonathan said nothing, but I was determined to wait him out. It took some time, but suddenly he slumped like the strings holding him up were cut all at once. I let go of one of his hands as he leaned back against the couch.

"We found out some shit about our father."

Okay. That wasn't totally shocking. I wouldn't have been surprised if that man's secrets had secrets. "Like what? Is he actually still alive?"

Jonathan chuckled, but the sound was hollow, devoid of any amusement. "That would be preferable so I could send him six feet under myself." The hand still covering mine curled, threading our fingers together. I allowed it, trying hard to ignore how nice it felt. "He had a secret safe with a bunch of documents inside."

I nodded, beckoning him to continue.

"It was no secret our father had mistresses. Hell, he might not have ever been faithful to our mother now that I really stop to think about it." Jonathan stared down at our clasped hands. His thumb moved in tight circles over the back of my hand. "The woman you saw was one of them."

I frowned. "But…I first saw her years ago."

"I know. That's probably why the bastard decided to fuck your family over," Jonathan replied before looking up at me. "The only other person we think knows was blackmailed into keeping the secret. We think he knew he couldn't do the same to you."

I frowned, trying to understand. "But I didn't even know who the woman was. I just thought she was some business associate or secretary. He never said anything to me."

"He wouldn't have wanted to take the chance probably. He got rid of you before you had a chance to know what you saw."

It was so out of the realm of normal, yet in the strangest of ways, it made sense. I had barely been introduced to the Dummonds when things had gone badly. Mrs. Dummond had been nice enough, but the senior Dummond had made me all sorts of uncomfortable. At the time, I just thought that maybe it was because he was my father's business partner, but now I wondered if my intuition was trying to tell me something.

"All this time, I spent years thinking that I did something," I said quietly. I had spent a decade angrily combing over every action I had taken, and none of it had been even close to correct.

"You did nothing wrong," Jonathan said firmly. He cupped my cheek. "I had thought he was just concerned with me taking up the mantle one day, but really he wanted to break us apart to cover his ass and hide his bastard child from being found out."

Holy shit. "Wait. You have another sibling?"

Jonathan sighed. "Yeah. A half-brother. All I know is that he's seventeen, and if I don't get married within the month, all my siblings and I will lose everything, and it will go to him."

It was like a record skipped, drawing me back to attention. "Wait. You have to get married otherwise... Is that why you asked me to marry you before?"

"No," he said, moving closer to me. "When I first asked you, that was all me."

"And now? It's to keep this kid from taking your place?"

"No!" he exclaimed, standing up from the couch. Jonathan paced the floor, but I was frozen in place. This was all too fucking much. I hadn't completely decided how I even felt about the direction we were going in. I had secured one of the locations I wanted, but I was still waiting to hear back from Anthony about the other. I was still navigating the Atlanta business scene. Marriage was on the table, but I'd thought I would have time to get ready. Time to get used to the fact that my hatred of Jonathan had been a cover for my hurt. Could I jump into marriage with him now and not regret it?

"I'm sorry I have to ask you again like this," Jonathan said, pulling my attention back to the newest dilemma. He was looking at me with an expression I didn't recognize. "I wanted to slowly court you so I could show you I'd changed. I wanted you to come to me willingly so I could show you just how good we could be."

The words were oddly sincere, and it was like seeing him in a new light. I had to concede that he had come through with every promise. He'd gotten me an in with some people and had my back when I needed it. So far, he was unobtrusive and such a good fuck that my legs shook just thinking about him. The feelings I'd had for him when we were younger still lingered and had begun to mature into something stronger than I had ever experienced. It was terrifying to think about giving myself over to the path we had embarked on, but I had to admit that when it came to relationships, I could do much worse. The man Jonathan had grown into was someone I could see by my side.

Fuck. I had no idea when it had happened, but slowly I had begun to fall even as I fought against it. I stared at him, wondering how that had even happened without me noticing. How had I missed the signs?

"I told my siblings you might not—"

"Let's do it."

He froze at my words, staring at me with confusion. "What? Regina, you don't have to."

I stood up from the couch and slowly walked toward him. "I know I don't have to," I replied. "But I still need you and your connections to build things up. I can't use those if you don't have them."

I could see disappointment in his eyes, and something in me didn't want to leave it like that between us.

"Not to mention you've grown on me. I kind of like you, Jonathan." Conceding that wasn't as painful as I thought it'd be, even if it was only a half-truth when it came to the strength of my feelings for him. "And I don't want your siblings to lose out on everything they worked for when it comes to dealing with your asshole of a dad."

Jonathan reached out, cupping my cheeks, and I stepped further into his orbit. "Please be very sure, Regina, because once I have you, I won't be able to let you go."

I lifted my hands to curl around his wrists. Leaning forward didn't feel like losing. When our lips brushed together, it felt a lot like winning. We had unfinished business, but I figured we could handle all that when we were married. I wasn't done with Jonathan, and I refused to give up now.

"Good."

Chapter Twenty-Three

Regina

My dress was perfect. Planning a wedding in one week had damn near been the death of both me and Jonathan, namely because I almost killed him. But now that we were here, I could concede this was a much better plan than going to the courthouse.

Jonathan's siblings had all pitched in their time to make this ceremony and reception as perfect as it could be on such short notice. The guest list had been one of the most rushed. We'd ended up inviting damn near anyone who wanted to attend, which was the one thing I was truly regretting.

"Liam, sit the fuck down."

I hadn't bothered to tell security to keep him out because I hadn't thought he would actually show his face—

a face still slightly swollen from the last time he and Jonathan met.

"No!" Liam objected. "She can't be seriously wanting to marry—"

"Shut up!" Alison hissed. Her expression was fierce, and I smiled happy she was able to come and have my back. Without her having kept me calm, I would have vibrated out of my skin before I even reached the aisle.

Soft murmurs started, and I damn near walked down to where Liam stood to beat him with my damn bouquet. My parents were seated right up front, and I could see my mom's horrified expression. They hadn't traveled at such short notice just to see me get arrested for smashing someone's face in.

"She doesn't know," Liam said, addressing the people around him before looking at me. "You don't know the kind of man he is! Not really."

Jonathan turned toward him, looking just as intimidating in his tuxedo as he had a week ago in the hallway of my condo. "He really wants me to knock his ass out."

I gripped Jonathan's hand and hoped that was enough to keep him from going after Liam. As much as I would have enjoyed watching him beat the bastard down, this was not the time for a fresh scandal. I had only just secured two locations, and things had started to calm down. The last thing we needed was rumors flying, considering my history with Liam and his influence.

"Jonnie," I whispered, hoping my words would fall on his ears only. "It's fine. Forget about him."

The tension was thick enough that it had the hairs on the back of my neck standing up. Security had finally made their way down the aisle, and though they were herding Liam out, his shouts still rang out with threats of consequences. I tried to ignore the looks from the crowd, though I was surprised to see Elizabeth staring after Liam with a disapproving frown. When I glanced at Christa, she had a hand over her mouth as she shook her head. When she saw I was looking, she mouthed for me not to worry. But how could I not? Liam had been a concern since he heard of Jonathan and my engagement. I had known he didn't approve, but I didn't think he would go so far as to crash the wedding he wasn't invited to. Fake or not, it was still my wedding day.

"I can't believe he'd show his ass in my presence," Jonathan hissed as he shifted to keep Liam in his line of sight. I squeezed his fingers tighter, though I knew if he really tried to break away, there wasn't much I could do outside of kneeing him in the dick. "I'm going to kill him this time."

His words weren't loud, but I knew everyone close enough could hear him. From her seat on the front row,

Casey nodded at me, and I shook my head. I didn't need her getting involved, not with her being pregnant. Ray wrapped an arm around her shoulders, but his gaze was rooted on Jonathan. I knew murder was clear on his face, but I had to get him in line somehow. Words didn't seem to be working, so I went with actions.

I slid back in front of him, not bothering to second-guess myself as I curled my arms around his neck and pressed a hard kiss against his lips. Audience or not, the feeling of his mouth on mine had my eyes closing and my body melting. No one else had ever made me feel like this—wild and yet so fucking free. When his arms wrapped around my back, I smiled against him, loving that even at his most murderous, I was the one who commanded his attention.

"Fuck. You can't keep doing that when you want to get your way," Jonathan groaned against my lips. His words were soft, but I could still hear the anger in them. I smirked.

"I didn't agree to that," I replied, loving his eyes on me. "Nowhere was it stated in the contract."

"I thought we were getting rid of the contract."

I hummed as I pretended to think. "Well, the only way we can do that is if this is for real."

I knew where he stood—had always known, really. It had just taken some time for me to figure out if that was where I wanted to be as well. It had been hard to admit that the feelings I had for Jonathan, while they'd warped and changed, had never gone away. The love I had for him when we were younger had been buried under the weight of his father's machinations, but Jonathan was not his father, and I refused to let that man win even in death.

"Is that what you want? Truly?" Jonathan asked as his gaze searched mine. The hope in his voice placated the part of me that still worried and waited for the other shoe to drop.

"It is," I replied steadily. "I want this. I want you."

Him tensing was the only warning I got before I was gathered in a tight embrace and twirled around. I clung to Jonathan's shoulders as I shouted in surprise. The world spun as my lips were again pressed against his, and I trusted him not to drop me as we slowly stopped.

"God, I love you."

Words I never thought I would hear coming from him slammed into me. But instead of being terrified, I only felt elated. A part of me felt cracked open and exposed, and I threw myself into the kiss, tasting Jonathan's love and giving him my own. It was scary and wonderful, and I felt it more deeply than the anger and rage that had sustained me for so long.

"Damnit, Jonnie," I gasped when we separated, neither of us moving too far from one another. "I love you and I can't believe I didn't see it before. You asshole, I think you broke me for anyone else."

The failed relationships. The dates that never grew into anything more. My decadelong obsession. All the signs had pointed to me not being over him, yet I had thought I only wanted revenge. How could I have not seen it?

"I'm sorry, baby." Jonathan shook his head before cupping my cheek. "If I hadn't been a coward, if I hadn't wanted to be like him—"

"Excuse me." We both turned to look at Jameson, having lost ourselves in one another. He was smiling widely, eyes dancing with amusement. "As happy as I am that you two are finally sorting your shit out, are we still doing this wedding thing or…"

"Yes," I said quickly before pushing Jonathan away slightly. "Yes, we are. Sorry."

He shook his head. "You two ridiculous kids are in love. I just wanted to say we could skip to the end since the kissing has already happened."

"Of course," Jonathan said, his hands sliding down to grip mine. He nodded at Jameson before looking back at me. "I do."

A few chuckles and laughter bubbled up from the crowd. Jameson snickered but didn't bother correcting him before turning to me. "And you? You sure you want to bind yourself to the trainwreck that is my big brother?"

I smiled and turned to Jonathan. "I do."

"Okay, then," Jameson said, voice still tinged with mirth. "I am happy to say that you are now man and wife. Kiss again and let's go so we can get this party started."

The crowd laughed, and though I knew things would be rough, I had eyes for only Jonathan. I was his and he was mine. This was inevitable, and I felt nothing but satisfaction that we had somehow gone through hell and found our way back to one another on the other side. Shit wouldn't be easy with Liam's threats lingering in the background and my long road to building back my family's legacy, but I didn't feel the weight of it all sitting on just my shoulders.

One of Jonathan's hands cupped my cheek, and I let myself lean into his touch. Kissing Jonathan was like coming home. It wasn't a weakness to want this. I could find strength in him and our love. I knew he would burn the world down for me, and I would happily do the same for him.

"Ladies and gentlemen, I present to you Mr. and Mrs. Jonathan and Regina Dummond."

Jameson's words pulled me out of the kiss before it turned not safe for audiences. Jonathan was smiling as he looked down at me. "Ready, Mrs. Dummond?"

I rolled my eyes but smiled. "Don't get too excited. I'm hyphenating it on paper."

"That's fine," he replied before offering me his arm as the processional music started. "I might do the same thing. Might be nice to be something other than just a Dummond."

I jerked my head toward him in surprise but let him lead me back down the aisle. By the time we were at the end and hidden by the bushes, my smile was wide enough to hurt.

"Don't you get tired of surprising me?"

Jonathan's arm slid from mine and wrapped around my waist, pulling me into the line of his body. It was a position I used to fight against, but now I leaned into him greedily, gobbling up every touch and enjoying how we fit so perfectly together.

"Never."

I snorted and shook my head. "Such an asshole." His lips were impossible to resist, and I vaguely noticed the photographer snapping a photo before pressing my lips against his.

Jonathan Dummond was an asshole, but he was mine.

AUTHOR'S NOTE

Thank you for reading *Passion Over Pride*. This family has a lot going on, and so many secrets have yet to be revealed. Jalissa might seem fun-loving, but she has a lot going on when it comes to either keeping things easy and casual or listening to her heart. Valerie won't wait around forever, and with a new player making themselves known, things are about to get even more complicated for the Dummond siblings.

As always, if you enjoyed this book and others I've written, please consider taking a moment to leave a review. Your support makes my writing possible!

ABOUT KARMEN LEE

Karmen Lee is an author of diverse and queer adult contemporary and steamy romance. She's a single mom living it up in Atlanta, Georgia with her kid, her cats, and humidity. When she's not carpooling or packing lunches, you can probably find her enjoying a glass of wine and dreaming up ways to show her readers a good time.

Never miss a New Release! Sign up for her newsletter: http://eepurl.com/g_UiEb

MORE BY KARMEN LEE

From Afterglow Books

The 7-10 Split: A Romantic Comedy (Out May 2024)

Dummond Siblings

Passion Over Power

Passion Over Pride

Coffee Shops of Love

Cups of You

Sips of Her

Tastes of Him

Open Road

Open Road: Coming Home (Out Fall/Winter 2024)

Sweet Heat Holiday Novellas

Her Christmas Wish

Standalone Novellas

Finding Forever With You

Only For The Night: A BWWM Sweet Temptations
Romance

Made in the USA
Columbia, SC
09 July 2024

38169484R10174